"You can't treat me like that, Steve Hall! You mind your own business!" I jabbed him in the ribs with my elbow.

"Now you're really asking for it!" I guess I must have hurt Steve, because he pinned my arms so that I couldn't move a muscle.

"Let me go!" I gasped.

His grip tightened and I yelped.

"Tell me you'll behave!"

"I will! I will! Let loose, you overgrown bear! If you don't let me go right now, I'm going to scream!"

"You would," he muttered in disgust. He was right. I was getting ready to, and took a deep breath.

The next thing I knew, Steve was kissing me.

Dear Readers:

Thank you for your many enthusiastic and helpful letters. In the months ahead we will be responding to your suggestions. Just as you have requested, we will be giving you more First Loves from the boy's point of view; and for you younger teens, younger characters. We will be featuring more contemporary, stronger heroines, and will be publishing, again in response to your wishes, more stories with bittersweet endings. Since most of you wanted to know more about our authors, from now on we will be including a short author's biography in the front of every First Love.

For our Book Club members we are publishing a monthly newsletter to keep you abreast of First Love plans and to share inside information about our authors and titles. These are just a few of the exciting ideas that First Love from Silhouette has in store for you.

Nancy Jackson
Senior Editor
Silhouette Books

JUST THE RIGHT AGE
Louise Chatterton

First Love from Silhouette

Published by Silhouette Books New York

America's Publisher of Contemporary Romance

SILHOUETTE BOOKS, a Division of Simon & Schuster, Inc.
1230 Avenue of the Americas, New York, N.Y. 10020

ISBN: 0-671-53392-4

First Silhouette Books printing April, 1984

10 9 8 7 6 5 4 3 2 1

To Wilma:
A Champion

JUST THE
RIGHT AGE

1

Grandma Fletcher let me have it when we were barely inside the door. I just set the groceries down on the kitchen table. It would be different if I had done something wrong, but I'd helped with the shopping in town the way I always do. When Grandma's mouth turns down, she's plenty mad.

"Linn, I'm too old for this nonsense with boys," she began. "I thought about it all the way home. It won't work. Sweetheart, it hurts me to say this, but I must."

"What is it, Grandma?"

"I believe the time has come for you to go to your mother."

I couldn't believe what I was hearing. Leave the farm. My grandpa and grandma, the two dearest people in the world. And my pony. How could she

9

say such a thing? "But Grandma, I don't want to leave. I've been here forever. You can't mean it."

"It won't do. I had a hard time raising your mother, and now it's starting all over."

"The boys weren't causing trouble."

"Linn, I'm not going to be trailed about in a grocery store by three absolute strangers who are trying to ogle my granddaughter."

"Why don't you tell *them?*"

"Because it's *you*. Those tank tops and your gold hair flying about will have every boy for miles around knocking at the door! Why, that one fellow must have been twenty if he was a day!"

"What am I supposed to do—disguise myself? Maybe I should develop a good case of acne."

"Linn, don't be ridiculous. There are ways to handle this, but I'm beyond trying. The answer is for you to go to your mother. She's young. She'll be understanding. I'm just an old fuddy-duddy."

"I like fuddy-duddies."

"You wouldn't very long, and I fear—it's best for you to go."

"You can't make me," I screamed. I knew she could, but I thought if I yelled loud enough she would give up. Her mouth tightened up a bit more, and she started toward the phone.

"Wait!" I was really desperate now. I grabbed the phone from her. I had to get the receiver because it's one of the push-button kind—the very latest, even though we live clear in southern Utah at Pepper Hill.

"Long distance calls cost a lot," I reminded her.

"Maybe you'd rather write." She reached for the receiver which I still held. "I have an idea." I didn't, but I thought something would come to mind if Grandma forgot about calling my mother. "Listen, Grandma, I'm going to do my hair in a braid, and I'll wear glasses, faded jeans and one of Grandpa's old shirts. I'll never look at boys. Scout's honor."

"Linn, you're not a Scout."

"I have to say something to make you believe me," I protested.

"I think you *would* try. But you can't stop yourself from growing up. Besides, you and your mother have been apart too many years. You hardly know each other. She's missing all the wonderful years of raising a daughter. You need each other. It won't be long before you're married and have a daughter of your own."

"You never said all that before. How come?"

"The time hasn't been right."

"For fifteen years the time is all wrong, but today it's right."

"You know as well as I do, your mother has been in and out of two marriages the past five years. I wanted to wait until things were more settled."

"And three strange guys settled it."

"Believe me child, you can't see it now, but trust me. It will be far better. A young girl needs a mother."

"She's not my mother. You are." I didn't want to hurt Grandma, but it was the plain truth. My mom never seemed to care about me at all. She came to visit the farm once or twice a year, but she spent all her time with Grandma. She hardly ever said "hello" to me. Well, maybe she said "hello."

Right then the kitchen door opened, and my grandpa came in. He'd been out in the barn with a new foal. We raise POAs, that's Pony of America. They're the ones with all the spots on the rump. We get really nervous before one is foaled because if they don't spot out, the selling price drops. This last one had spots sprinkled all over. It was my pony's foal, a midnight black like her mother.

I relaxed a little to know Grandpa was there. He's kind of gruff, but he doesn't mean anything by it.

"What you two hollering about in here?" he asked with a twinkle in his eye.

"Grandpa, you don't want me to go live with Mom, do you?" I thought I'd get my arguments in first so Grandma wouldn't have a chance.

"Serious as all that?" he questioned as he stroked his whiskers a little and sat down at the kitchen table. He started buttering some of Grandma's homemade bread. You could tell he was playing for time. He's pretty smart all right.

"Henry, the time has come to face facts," Grandma said as she sat opposite him. I hung back by the fridge, waiting. "Linn's growing up now, and she's getting to be a handful. I don't have to remind you what it's like, with boys calling at all hours, and pacing the floor wondering if a child's ever going to come home. We're too old for all that, Henry."

I thought Grandma was being unfair saying I

would be out late at night. I always came home by ten, but I knew better than to argue. Seemed to me she was worrying over nothing. Maybe Grandpa thought so too, because he leaned over and patted her shoulder.

"So what do you have in mind, Mama?" he asked.

"It would be good for Linn to be with Carol. They've never had a chance to get to know each other. Carol is young and will show Linn the way."

"You're talking about sending my ranching partner away."

"But it's best all around. We'll miss her, but in the end she'll be happier. Henry, three men had the gall to follow us about in Burton's Grocery. That wasn't all. On the way home another young man nearly ran us off the road because he was staring at Linn and not putting his mind to his driving."

"Didn't know you were so deadly, youngster." Grandpa chuckled.

"She makes it sound awful, Grandpa. Don't believe her. Grandma wasn't watching where she was going for some reason, and we had to swerve at the last minute."

"Come here, tadpole." Grandpa calls me that because as a kid I hunted tadpoles when we went fishing in the mountains. I moved close to Grandpa and put my arm around his shoulder, but I knew already. He tried to make it easier. "Youngster, appears you're kinda growing up on us. Now, your grandma knows best. I'm not going against her."

It was useless to say anything. I sat down while

Grandma made the call. It didn't take a mind reader to know that my mom wasn't anxious to get me either.

"Yes, Carol," Grandma said, "but you could put her up on your sofa until you make other arrangements." There was a long pause, and then Grandma said, "We know you don't make lots of money, but we feel this is important. After all, she is your daughter." Guess my mom couldn't understand all the fuss. That didn't stop Grandma. "We'll bring her up for the start of school. . . . All right. . . . We'll see you then. Love you. . . . Bye."

I didn't wait for grandma to tell me what they said. I ran out the back door and across the grass to the path that led to the barn. I jumped the irrigation ditch and ducked through the plum trees. The branches slapped and scratched at me, but I didn't pay attention. I tasted salt from my tears as I jerked open the barn door and slammed it behind me. I ran straight for Starlight's stall. There was no need to wait for my eyes to get used to the dark after being in the bright sun because I had been here so many times.

Starlight was at the door of her stall, and I put my arms around her neck and bawled all over her mane. She didn't mind. I told Starlight how awful everything was. About Grandma wanting to get rid of me, and Grandpa letting her do it, and my mom not caring. I cried until I started to hiccup.

As usual, I had no handkerchief. I sniffed and brushed away the tears with my arms. I sighed as I got a handful of grain from the feed bag and held it for my pony. Her lips tickled my hand as she nuzzled it.

Grandpa kept all our equipment handy in the tack room, and I went to get brushes. Brushing Starlight felt comforting. It made me forget. She wasn't a bit nervous that I was in the stall with her foal. I tried to think of a name. "Twilight" sounded right.

As I brushed long strokes on Starlight's silky coat, memories kept nagging at me. Like when I was a kid and asked about my dad. Grandma said he was gone long before I was born. That was all. I never saw a picture of him. Nothing. Grandma told me lots about Mom. She was smart and pretty. She had to leave to get a job. There weren't any at Pepper Hill. I remembered my mom as the beautiful lady who brought me presents. Grandma was always telling me to say "hello" to her or to thank her. I felt funny. I didn't know her, and I could never think of anything to say.

When I was nine, I heard Grandma and Grandpa talking one night. They were saying I should go to Salt Lake. I cried a lot that night. I found out later Mom was getting married. I never heard any more about it. The next time Mom came, she cried forever. Grandma told me things didn't work out for Mom.

After that I never worried about going with my mom. She got married again, but Grandma didn't say anything to me about leaving. Not until today.

I never thought about Grandma being old. I guessed she was. Her hair was almost all white. She could be grouchy, but not very often. She scared me now. I didn't know if she loved me.

I heard the barn door open and Grandpa whistling. I kept brushing Starlight.

"You all right, tadpole?"

"Sure, Grandpa."

"You'll be fine." I stopped brushing and unlatched the stall. I stepped outside, closing the door carefully behind me. Grandpa stood there with his arms hanging at his sides, watching. I couldn't be sure, but I thought tears gathered in his eyes. I heard him breathing in short gasps. *I'd better be brave for both of us,* I told myself.

"Grandpa?" I whispered. He didn't answer, but kind of swallowed. "What's going to happen to me? I'm scared to think about tomorrow. What will happen after that . . . oh, Grandpa." I threw my arms around his waist and buried my face in his chest.

"Beyond tomorrow, tadpole, is the rest of your life, sort of a magical dream if you make it so." I clung to Grandpa. He hugged me for a long time.

August came too soon. Grandpa and Grandma drove me to Salt Lake in their new truck. It was quiet most of the way. Finally, Grandma thought of something to say.

"Carol said she was able to get a house. It has two bedrooms, so you'll have your own room." I didn't answer. I had my own room back at the farm.

The drive took most of the day. We started out at six in the morning and then had breakfast in Cedar.

The sun was burning down when we turned off the freeway on thirteenth South and made our way through the traffic to the residential area.

And then I saw my "new" house. Wow, what a mess! Only patches of white paint remained on what must have been a white house at one time. The lawn waved like wheat.

As soon as we pulled in the drive, Mom came out the front door. She was as I remembered her, blond hair all fluffy and green eyes like mine. She wore a black shirt and pants. Pretty glamorous for a mom.

"Hi Mother, Dad," she called. "Hello, Linn."

"Hi," I answered as I climbed out of the truck, all the time keeping my eyes on my sneakers.

"Where should I put Linn's things?" Grandpa asked as he lifted my cases from the bed of the truck. Mom waved him inside. Grandma gave my mom a hug, and she motioned for me to do the same. I turned and followed Grandpa into the house.

Something smelled like moldy cheese, but after a while I didn't notice it anymore. Guess my mom was pretty poor, because the light in the front room was a bare bulb, and stuffing dribbled out of the couch in a couple of places. The green shag rug gave me a queasy feeling. I hurried after Grandpa into my bedroom.

White curtains hung at the window with a little chest to one side. A cot was the bed, and I plumped down on it. It rocked a little, but it was soft, and the blankets would keep me warm.

Grandpa set my cases down. He had his hands

on his hips, looking at things and muttering to himself. "This won't be bad, tadpole," he said.

"Ya, fine." I didn't know what else to say.

Grandma and Mom crowded in. I couldn't move off the bed, so I just sat.

"Oh, this is so feminine, Carol. Perfect." She used more words like *quaint* and *sweet* to describe my room. She went on to explain to me how many neighbors we would have, and I could make friends with girls my own age.

"Will you stay for dinner?" Mom asked.

"We gotta be getting back," Grandpa replied. My heart sank. It would have been so much easier if they had stayed. Grandpa headed out the door.

"You do what your mom says," Grandma instructed, as she patted me on the head and gave me a hug. Then they were gone. Grandpa forgot to kiss me good-bye.

I decided the best thing to do was unpack. It would keep me occupied for a little while. Mom offered to help, but I told her there wasn't that much. She sat on the cot, and I put things away.

I had a picture of Grandma and Grandpa that I put on the chest. My favorite was a picture of Starlight and me. I guessed I wouldn't see Starlight for a long time.

"I hope you'll like it here," Mom said. "I moved in a couple of days ago, so there's still a lot to do."

"It's fine."

The next few days Mom and I didn't talk much unless she told me to do something. Even when we ate, it was quiet. I found out she isn't home that much. She goes to work at the phone company at seven in the morning, and I don't see her again until six at night. At first I thought I'd be lonely, but then I decided it was almost like having a house of my own. Some house. It needed fixing, but Mom didn't own any tools.

Another thing, lots of creatures lived in the house besides me. At night I could hear mice running back and forth in the ceiling. I really hated the scratching and scraping.

It wouldn't hurt, I thought, to use a little of the money Grandma gave me for traps and poison. There was a corner grocery a couple of blocks away. The people lived right at the store. It reminded me of home—I mean the farm. I bought some stationery and envelopes, too.

How to get in the attic? I circled the house on the outside and discovered a small door near the roof. I'd need a ladder. Jeez. I sat down on the steps to figure. Grandpa said never borrow. When you have everything, that advice works. The neighbors to the east were my choice. The Haights. Someone had been peeking out the window at me earlier. If they were curious, I'd go meet them. But how to get up the nerve?

As I walked up the Haights' front steps, a little kid came running out of the house with a water pistol and squirted me.

"Bang! Bang!" he shouted and then giggled.

"Augh!" I gasped and clutched my stomach. Then I staggered a little. The kid stopped and gaped, openmouthed. My death scene was interrupted by Mrs. Haight. I didn't even get a chance to knock at the door.

"Dougie, what have you been doing?" she scolded. Turning to me, she said, "Don't mind Dougie. He's the youngest and spoiled to pieces. Goodness, you're wet."

"A little damp," I said with a smile. I was already planning a revenge, maybe a water fight with hoses. Though Dougie was pretty small. He couldn't have been more than six.

"I'm Karlene Haight. Come on in."

"Thanks. My name's Linn. Linn Romney."

"It surely is a relief to have someone in that house after all this time. I hope you plan to stay."

To myself I thought how much I wanted to be with Grandpa and Grandma. It really was my greatest wish not to stay at all. If I left, Mom could go back to an apartment. Better not make Mrs. Haight think we'd be permanent.

"We're not exactly sure how long we'll stay," I said.

Mrs. Haight walked back in the kitchen, and the smell of bread almost brought tears to my eyes.

"Sit right there. I'm making cinnamon rolls. You'll have some?"

"Thanks." My mouth watered as I gazed at the dripper pan with lightly frosted rolls snuggled inside. Mrs. Haight treated me so well. Maybe she'd let me borrow the ladder.

I sipped some cold milk and turned my attention to the roll. Unwinding the rolls a little at a time made them last longer. It'd be nice if Mom had time to make some rolls. She was always too tired when she got home. I should have learned to do it, but I hated being inside the house. I felt better working in the yard. When the roll was gone, I craved more. I wouldn't ask. I figured it was better to keep Mrs. Haight in a good mood so she'd let me take the ladder.

"I never did find out your mom's name." Mrs. Haight's voice jerked me back to the present.

"Carol—Carol Neever."

"The two of you look so much alike with your blond hair. Your mom works such long hours that I haven't had a chance to talk to her at all."

"I don't see much of her myself. That's why it's pretty much up to me to straighten up around the place."

"That old house needs repairs. With a little work it will be respectable," she encouraged.

"I'm trying to get rid of the mice right now," I confided.

"Aren't they a nuisance?"

"Keep me awake. The bed is strange to me, too. I keep waking up and wondering where I am, so that probably has something to do with it."

"You'll get used to it, but not the mice."

"That's why I came over," I began before thinking. Now she would think me a pest. "And to get to know you, too," I added hastily.

"What do you need?" Mrs. Haight laughed, and her eyes crinkled at the corners. Mrs. Haight was a big, friendly woman; I liked her. I liked her a lot. I felt I could tell her almost anything, and we had barely met.

I blurted what was on my mind. "I need a ladder. I'm going to set out traps and poison in the attic."

"There's one out back in the garage. You be careful, Linn. It might be slow work getting that yard cleaned up with a broken leg."

"Don't worry," I said.

"Get Dougie to help you."

"Dougie?" I asked skeptically.

"He'll think it's an adventure. He's been peeking at you all morning. You're his new playmate."

"Boys really take to me," I said with a grin.

"I can see why. You're the only one who dies when you're shot." She chuckled. "You'll be a good diversion for him. Naturally, I don't expect you to let him pester you, but if you tease with him a little, I'll be grateful. There aren't any friends his age on the block."

"I haven't seen anyone my age either."

"I don't think there is anyone. People around here are getting older. Their families are gone. My children are all married except Dougie. He's my surprise package."

I didn't know what to say to that. I thought it time to leave. "I better get to work. Thanks for the rolls and the ladder."

"You come right over whenever you need anything. We'll help you get settled. I surely don't envy your mom working those long hours. For myself, I like being home."

Twice Mrs. Haight said how hard Mom worked. Maybe I ought to do a little more around the house. Mrs. Haight might be sorry she said to come over, because I was looking forward to the next time I would see her.

She was right. Dougie was hopping around waiting to see what I'd do. I told him to get on the other end of the ladder, and he acted as though I had given him an ice-cream cone.

I put the ladder against the side of the house as Dougie pelted me with questions.

"Whatcha doing that for? Can I go up? You giving our ladder back? My dad'll be mad if you keep it. Can I help carry it back?"

I told him I was setting traps, and he couldn't come because he'd get hurt, and yes, I would take the ladder back. Dougie thought he should steady the ladder, and I told him he could, as long as he didn't climb up. He promised to mind.

When I got up to the attic, it was dark. I called down to Dougie. "Hey, Dougie. It's dark up here. Go ask your mom for a flashlight."

"Okay." His voice sounded excited, and I smiled. Little kids don't mind doing the oddest things. I climbed down the ladder about halfway to wait for him.

A car honked, and I turned. It stopped right in front. A boy got out. There are boys, and there are *boys*. This one had dark curly hair, and his shirt was open down the front so you could see how tan he was. He had lots of black hair on his chest.

I supposed this was the kind of boy Grandma was scared I would like. Was she ever right! I squinted down at him because the sun was in my eyes. He walked straight over to the ladder.

"Say, that's kind of dangerous. Need some help?"

"Uh uh."

"You're new around here," he said.

23

"Uh huh." I said before, I'm not much at conversation. I can never think of what to say.

"What're you doing?"

Should I tell the truth? Did I want him to know that this run-down place had mice—maybe even rats? Of course, it could be squirrels or birds. Who could tell? I would be better off to say something else. Perhaps I could be installing a TV antenna? He would never believe it. Best to just get rid of him. Dougie would be back any minute. He would surely tell Mom that a strange boy was here. Then Mom would write Grandma, and Grandma would be glad she didn't have to put up with me.

"I'm thinking," I finally answered.

"Can I help?" he grinned. He had white, even teeth.

"You good at it?" I asked skeptically.

"Try me." He smiled.

"Who wrote the Declaration of Independence?" I could have asked him something easier, like two and two, but I had to get him out of here quick.

"Thomas Jefferson. So now what are you going to do?" He figured he had me cornered, and he was right.

"Listen, do you have a name?"

"Steve Hall. What's yours?"

"Linn Romney, spelled with an *i*. Steve, I'm doing some secret work up here, so I appreciate the offer, but no thanks."

"I love secrets. I never tell. You can trust good, old Steve."

"No, this is even a bigger secret than that. Sorry. You live around here?" This really was not the way

24

to make him leave, but at least I changed the subject.

"Couple of blocks east."

The rest of what he said was drowned out by Dougie's piercing voice. "Linn, Linn, I got it. Mom let me take the flashlight." Dougie came running across the yard with the flashlight clutched in his fist. "Here, Linn. Steve!" Dougie forgot the flashlight immediately, and I soon withdrew my outstretched hand. "You come to see me?" That Dougie was never at a loss. He went right over to Steve, and got his hair tousled for his efforts.

"Sure thing, buddy."

"Mom has cinnamon rolls," Dougie enticed.

"I can see I picked the right day."

"I'm helping Linn set traps," Dougie announced proudly, and I nearly fell off the ladder.

"You better give me the flashlight then." I knew when I saw Dougie's face fall I'd said the wrong thing. "Sorry, Dougie. I'm just being crabby. You've been great to help." He brightened a little. I prayed Steve would leave. Obviously he had figured out exactly what I was doing on the ladder.

"Dougie," Steve said, "how'd you like a ride in my car?"

"Boy! Would I!" Now I really was ashamed. Steve was making up to Dougie for my rudeness. Why would he take such an interest in a little kid?

As if he'd read my thoughts, he explained. "Karlene's my aunt. I visit them once in a while. Dougie's my copilot in our rocket ship."

"That the rocket ship parked at the curb?" I asked as Dougie handed up the flashlight.

"You bet. She travels at 150 light-years a second."

Dougie started pulling on Steve's shirt, but he stood his ground.

"You going to East?"

"Sure."

"What year are you?"

"First."

"Oh, you mean sophomore." How could I know what they called it around here? My hands tightened on the ladder. I was getting all worked up because here, not two feet from me, was the most stunning boy I'd ever talked to. Not only was I in my boy-repellent clothes, but I was setting mousetraps. At least I should try to remember my manners as my grandmother so often reminded me.

"What year are you?"

"Senior. It's going to be a great year. We'll take State in at least four sports—maybe five."

"Are you on the teams?" What an inane question, I thought—a blind person could tell he was the star of all of them.

"I'm on the weight team, and I play a little football. We've started practice. Our first game is next Friday."

"I'll be sure to watch for you."

Dougie wrestled one of Steve's legs, but he maintained his position by the ladder with little effort. "See you, too. Maybe before Friday." Steve leaned down and picked up Dougie. He heaved him in the air with one hand like a prize trophy. "Come on, partner. You're holding us up. We need

26

to get this ship off the launch pad." Dougie squealed.

"Dougie, don't forget to come back in the next century to help with the ladder," I called after them.

With that, the two space cadets were launched in their ship, and I returned to the attic to face the more harrowing task of baiting mousetraps.

I tried not to think about Steve. I was going back to the farm, and nothing would stop me. Not even Steve Hall.

2

I gave regular doses of poison to the mice. I'm sure it fattened them up. It was hopeless, but the trap caught a few. I checked every day. It was a drag asking Mrs. Haight for her ladder, and I worried that she would get fed up with me. She always smiled and told me to get it, though. At least I bought my own flashlight.

One afternoon I was sitting on my cot writing my fourth letter to Grandma and Grandpa. (I wrote one every day.) They hadn't answered my first letter yet. I knew it was futile to think they'd let me come back. Even though I'd told them boys were no bother and I would do everything Mom said, what was the use? That reminded me, Mom had said to clean up the house and get dinner started, but this house was too gloomy to stay in. My room was an exception. Anyway, I was just finishing the

28

letter when I heard a snap followed by a squeaking. I bounced off the bed in a hurry and grabbed the flashlight. I ran to the Haights'. I didn't bother to ask for the ladder but went straight to the garage.

When I finally crawled in the attic and flicked on the light, I could see a mouse dragging the trap after him. His leg was caught. I watched, fascinated but a little sick. Then he started to chew on his leg. I gritted my teeth and scrambled over to the mouse. I snatched the trap and flung it out the open attic door. Tears started, but I blinked them away. I had to get something to kill the mouse.

Back down in the yard I scanned around for a rock, but saw nothing. I ran in the house. The broom! Outside, the mouse dragged the trap across the grass in an effort to get away. I took the broom handle and aimed. Yuk!

To get my mind off the mouse business I visited Mrs. Haight. She was putting up peaches. She handed me a paring knife. We worked and talked.

"Our lawn grows by the minute. Doesn't look like Mom will be getting a mower."

"Honey, you don't need a mower. A herd of sheep would be more like it," Mrs. Haight said as she poured syrup over the bottled peaches.

"Know anybody with a goat? He could chew up the old shoes and cans as well as the grass."

"Linn, it seems to me—and I'm not trying to force work on you—but if you get some garbage bags and go around the yard, you could gather up all the trash and put it out front. I'll call the City Cleanup to pick it up."

"Why didn't I think of that?"

"You would have. When the yard's clean, come get our mower."

"That grass is long. It might wreck the mower."

"It's an old mower. Nothing could hurt it. No gas in it, though."

"I'll get the gas." I was so excited to begin work on our yard, I could barely wait until we put the batch of peaches in the cold packer.

"Dougie! Dougie!" I yelled as I finally ran out the front door and down the steps. "Come on! We're going treasure hunting."

That did it. Dougie was playing in the sandpile in the front yard. He threw down his spoon and came running. "We gonna find gold and silver?"

"Lots better stuff than that. We'll have a prize for the best find," I said breathlessly as I ran in the front door of my house to get the garbage bags.

In the next hour Dougie and I found various treasures. Plenty of sneakers, old cans, broken bottles. Dougie found two rubber balls and a baseball, and we had fun watching ants scramble to get their grubs to a safe place when I lifted up an old board. We also found a whistle that didn't work, and a horseshoe—in the middle of the city!

We hauled everything out front, including dead tree limbs and a set of rusted mattress springs. Poor Dougie was so dirty and tired I didn't think he could stand, let alone walk. But he made it over to Arctic Circle just fine for me to buy him a frostee. We stopped at the station on the way back for a gallon of gas.

The mower seemed like a relic from the Spanish-American War. It looked as though it might fall apart of old age, and it would be my head, I thought; but after seven pulls of the starter and some cuss words that I won't repeat (I made sure Dougie wasn't within earshot), the mower started. I even figured a way of lifting it up in front and letting it down slowly on the waist-high grass. It did take a while, but it cut. Mom sure would be surprised.

As I finished one side and moved to the other, I caught sight of Steve's car out of the corner of my eye. My head snapped up, so I had a chance to see Steve with a girl. She had dark hair. They were pressed up so close that from a distance I couldn't see more than one person. It took me a minute to figure, but I guess they were both sitting in one seat.

Somehow I couldn't get excited about cutting the grass after that, but I still worked at it. I had nearly finished when I realized someone was watching me. On the walkway, straddling a ten-speed, was a girl about my own age. If she had been one of Dougie's martians, I couldn't have been more surprised.

She grinned at me, so I smiled a little and shut off the motor.

"Hi," I said. "You live around here?" I almost prayed for her to say she did.

"Over on Green Street. I'm Patty Varow."

"Linn Romney. How come you're over here?"

"Bike ride. You have a bike?"

"Down home. Maybe I should send for it, but then I don't know how long I'll be here."

"Where's *down home?*"

"Pepper Hill. Southern Utah."

31

"Jeez, this place will never look the same without the forest."

"Yeh, but we have to see daylight now and then. Where do you go to school, Patty?"

"East."

"Really? What year?"

"First."

"Oh, you mean sophomore." I felt pretty smug. Here was someone my speed. Maybe it wouldn't be so bad. I pronounced *sophomore* with a stress on the second *o,* just the way Steve had done.

As we were talking, I saw Mom coming down the street from the bus stop. Patty's gaze followed mine, and she moved a little so Mom could get by. I thought Mom did a double take when she saw all the garbage stacked up out front. I introduced Patty, and then Mom went in the house.

I turned to Patty. I'd been thinking about school. This was the perfect chance. "Don't suppose you'd like to go with me to school on the first day?" I felt embarrassed to ask on such short acquaintance, but it might be my only opportunity. I had met absolutely no one my own age, and school would be opening next Wednesday.

"Are you registered?" Patty asked.

"I'm not," I admitted.

"Why don't we go over tomorrow afternoon and get you registered? You probably need your report cards from last year or something. Do you have a transfer?"

I guessed Patty thought I was pretty stupid. I never thought to ask the school for anything. I had my report card, but that was it. "I'll find something," I said. I'm pretty good at faking it, but a sick feeling inside told me East would find some reason not to let me in.

We were deciding on a time when Mom came to the door. She had one hand on her hip, and she wasn't smiling.

"Linn, would you come in here?"

"Gotta go. See you tomorrow." I waved at Patty and smiled, but I didn't feel much like it. I had forgotten to clean up the house and get dinner ready. The lecture started before I got inside the door.

"Linn, I don't ask you to do much. Look at this place! When I leave instructions, I expect them to be carried out."

"Sorry." I thought about my letter to Grandma telling how I always did everything Mom said. Wait till they heard from her now!

"Why don't you lie down and rest for a few minutes while I get things started," I suggested, in hopes she'd calm down. I heard her mutter something like "what's the use" as she walked into her bedroom and shut the door.

The next day, I registered. The school is on what they call a "modular" system. Students work at their own speed, and classes are taught in blocks of time, so I'd be going at different times depending on the day. After looking at my report card, the counselor said I would fit into the advanced art class and asked if I wanted to sign up. Far out. The rest of the classes were the usual.

I was glad Patty went with me. When the counselor, Mrs. Pettigrew, found out we were friends and I was new in town, she put me in a couple of Patty's classes. The counselor said we had all these choices, but it seemed as though everyone took pretty much the same thing.

At dinner I started to tell Mom about what had happened that day. "I registered for school today," I mentioned between mouthfuls of spaghetti with my homemade sauce.

"That's nice." She frowned at me so I didn't want to say more.

"Something wrong with that?" I finally asked.

"You do everything for yourself, don't you? Never ask. Never let me in on a thing. Just go ahead. I thought *parents* registered their kids."

"Not in high school, for cripes sakes."

"All the same, I don't know why we even bother. We don't talk. You don't ask me about things. You go around looking like something out of *Tom Sawyer*."

"But I like looking like this." That was a lie. I wore baggy clothes so there wouldn't be any problem with boys, and Grandma would take me back.

"I try to set a good example, but every day the same T-shirt and jeans. Do you think a boy will be interested in a girl who dresses like that?"

"Who says I want boys staring at me?" I wondered whose side she was on.

"You are the strangest. What did Ma teach you down there on that farm anyway? I should have checked."

"Grandma did just fine," I exploded.

"Not from where I sit."

"You're mad because you have to take care of me, and you're ashamed of my looks."

"People will laugh. Remember, this isn't Pepper Hill. I shudder to think what it's like down there. It's been so long. How I ever loved the place, I'll never know."

I couldn't believe her. Every time I think of it I still get mad. I wanted to hit her with something. "The farm is the most wonderful place in the whole world," I shouted, "and a stupid house like this isn't worth having. I'd rather live on the street."

"For all I care, Linn, you can do just that. I work hard to pay for this place. I did have a nice apartment, furnished, until you were forced on me. Don't think I love it here. There was a swimming pool and tennis court at my old apartment. Now I have a *family*. Things are lots different for me, too."

"Then go back to wherever you came from. Don't let me keep you."

"I wish I could."

"What's stopping you? I'm not." I jumped up from the table and slammed out of the house. It was better when we didn't try to talk to each other. We didn't even like each other much.

After my temper cooled, I realized I didn't have anyplace to go. I decided to head over to the park and jog a while. Things were going crazy; I couldn't stay around the house.

There was no way I'd ever be happy again. Mom

hated me. Grandma thought I was a pain. Poor Grandpa. Too bad I had to go on living someplace, I thought.

Jogging took my mind off things. I followed a worn path all the way around the park. It was getting dark, but lots of people still remained. Some jogged. Fellows polished their cars. Teenagers laughed and played on the swings and bars. A blond boy worked out on the rings. He was all concentration as he did a cross and handstands.

The lights from the tennis courts were like a beacon, and I trotted over to watch the play. I don't play tennis, but I had watched matches on TV.

I wandered up and down the alleys between the courts, about twenty of them. I watched two older men playing. They took their time and sliced the ball a lot, but the ball skimmed the net at times, too. One wore an old, battered hat, but his most distinguishing feature was his gray-and-black mustache and beard. I moved on down the row by the pro shop. My heart started pounding. In the far court, number 8, Steve was playing with a red-headed guy. I ached to stroll by and casually watch the game, but how obvious could I get? He'd know for sure I was interested. I was so different. Sickening to be one of a crowd of worshipers. I stood a court away, hoping he wouldn't notice.

Strange, that I'd never seen anything very interesting about a boy. Now my eyes were glued to Steve as though my life depended on it.

Both Steve and his friend were wearing whites, although Steve filled his out better. The redhead was the stringy sort; he was serving. Wow, he served hard, but the ball caught the tape. He sliced the second ball. I held my breath, but Steve returned it easily, whipping the ball down the line. The redhead barely saved the point with a lob, but Steve rushed the net and finished it off. Both boys laughed and started to change sides of the net.

Then Steve saw me. "Hi," he called.

"Hi," I said in confusion, and waved a little. The boys turned back to their game, and I stumbled toward the pro shop. If I could only play tennis!

The pro shop door stood open invitingly. After a slight hesitation, I mounted the two steps and went inside. A glass display case held rackets, balls, presses and other equipment. Nearby, an oriental young man sat at a machine stringing a racket. It was the first time I'd ever seen such a device. He glanced up.

"Can I help you?"

"I'd like—to look," I said with a sigh. I could see the price tags on the rackets. The fifty dollars grandma gave me seemed like a fortune at the time. Now, I realized it wasn't anywhere nearly enough. I'd get a racket some way.

"I'd like to take some tennis lessons," I said.

"County Rec is over for the summer," he replied. "You'd have to go to one of the clubs. Cottonwood has a pretty good deal."

"Sure. Thanks." So tennis wasn't my thing. My mind wouldn't let it go. I kept seeing myself on a court with Steve.

Defeated, I turned to leave. I was startled to see it was pitch dark outside. I didn't want to run, but it felt better than dragging along. As I got closer and closer to home, my legs wouldn't move fast.

I straggled up the walk and saw the mower right where I left it. With a guilty start I wheeled it over to the Haights' and put it in the garage. Lucky it wasn't stolen. Then again, who would want it?

I couldn't put off going in the house any longer. I took a deep breath and went inside.

"Where have you been?" Mom glared at me and took a few steps toward me. She raised her hand, and I thought she would hit me. Her hand dropped.

"Jogging over at the park."

"Let me tell you, young lady, I've been worried half out of my mind. I thought you had run away."

"Sorry." Run away? Who would want a spare fifteen-year-old kid? "Where would I go?"

"I thought you might be crazy enough to hitch a ride back to the farm."

"They'd just send me back." For a minute I don't think Mom knew what to say. Finally, she sighed.

"We better sit down and talk."

Wasn't that just the way! Talking had caused all the trouble. Now she wanted to talk some more. Not me. "Nothing to say."

"There are a few home truths you'd better hear. Let's sit on the couch."

"I can stand." I sounded pretty ornery, but if we sat, it would be easy to start another fight. I hate fights.

"You'll sit. Now." I sat. I thought if I concentrated on something else—like Starlight—she wouldn't make me so mad. She still came through loud and clear. "There are a couple of things we need to get straight. First, you don't go anywhere without telling me where you are going and when you'll be back. Second, you don't go out after dark alone. Most important, you *never* smart mouth me."

Better that I didn't talk. She'd say I was *smart mouthing*. I kept staring at a hole in the rug. Parents can be a pain sometimes. Her rules were fair enough, but she acted as though I didn't obey. When a person is mad, rules don't count. I hadn't been thinking about how Mom would be worried. I'd wanted to get away quickly. Running in the park had felt good. It took the hurt away, at least some of it.

"Linn, what do you have to say for yourself?"

"Nothing."

"You'd better come up with something because you're going to be grounded for a week if you don't."

"I can't promise not to leave again. I don't know what will happen. I'll try, but when I'm upset I don't think straight."

"That's just an excuse for not doing what you're told," she said. "No wonder Ma had such a time with you."

"I never ran away from Grandma. She was always good to me."

"Let me hear you say that I've been mean. It would be a lie. Hey, listen—I gave up my bowling league the past two weeks for you. Yes, I did. I had a substitute so I could stay home with my little girl."

"I don't need anybody to babysit me."

"Linn, I'm trying to be your mother."

"Mothers don't babysit their teenage kids."

"If it's all right with you, next Wednesday I'll be bowling."

Imagine! She blamed me because she didn't go bowling. It would be different if we had done something fun. We cleaned the living room and listened to the radio.

"Fine with me."

"On second thought, maybe I shouldn't. You'll be off running around. I better keep an eye on you. Another thing, what do you intend to do with all that trash in the front yard?"

"The garbage men will pick it up."

"Garbage day is Monday. We have to look at that for three more days. Besides, they won't take it. Next time ask before you go ahead."

Jeez. What could I say? Mom's face was getting red. I could see we were in for another fight. "Don't worry. I promise to stay home and be good when you're out on Wednesday. I'll take care of the trash, too." Tell them what they want to hear, I thought. Yeah, I learned fast.

"I've had enough for tonight. Better phone Ma and let her know you're home."

"Why would she care?" All these calls back and forth were driving me nuts.

"When you left, I called her. I told her you ran away, and I didn't know what to do. She told me to call the police."

My mouth dropped, and I stared. Police. Grandma. What a mess! For sure I wouldn't be going back to the farm. "You must hate me to run right to Grandma. What will she think?"

"But I was worried."

"So you get Grandma all upset, too? She's sure to think the worst. Thanks a lot."

"Linn, you act as though it were my fault."

"You called."

"And you ran away," Mom accused.

"But I didn't. I jogged around the park a couple of times and came home."

"How was I to know that?"

"If you knew me at all or cared about me, you wouldn't have to ask."

"At least I didn't call the police." I guess Mom wanted credit for a little sense, but there was no way.

"Yes, that's something. I wonder if the police are worried about what kind of a kid I am. I'm going to bed."

"I'll call your grandmother. Sure you don't want to talk?"

"I don't have anything to say. You said it all."

3

For the first day of school I met Patty over on Ninth, and we took the bus together. I had a new blouse but faded jeans, and I still did my hair down the back in a French braid. I even used a little lip gloss. Patty was wearing a beige skirt and flowered blouse. Makeup was pretty much a mystery to me, but I could tell she had mascara and eyeliner on, besides the lip gloss.

I felt shaky inside as we walked up the front steps. I already knew where my classes and locker were, so the kids were my only problem.

"Hi, Patty." A voice floated by as we pushed past a group of students who were standing around talking.

"Hi, Patty." Again. Seems as though everybody knew Patty.

"Hey, come on over. I want you to meet some-

42

body," Patty called back. The girls walking toward us had to be auditioning for "Charlie's Angels." From the perfection of their clothes, hair, makeup and nails I knew they had been up long before dawn preparing for their big scene. I glanced down at my jeans and felt a little sick. What the heck. I told myself it was okay. I was going to stick to what I said. Then, I saw a girl in jeans. I felt a little better until someone mentioned they were designer jeans.

I was miserable as Patty made the introductions. "Karen and Sheena, this is Linn Romney. She's from southern Utah, a little place called Pepper Hill."

"Hi," the girls chorused. Karen had long brown hair that curled around her face. Sheena's hair was darker, but it was long, too.

"Anybody for trying out for cheerleader or something?" Karen asked. I'd have bet she wouldn't need to try. The other girls would take one look at her and give up.

"There aren't tryouts. That was last year," Patty said. Everybody argued, but it wasn't any use. It was true. Pep Club, too. We'd have to wait until the end of the year. I didn't have any hopes, but Karen and Sheena—it was a shame.

"Guess it's up to the sophomores to keep up studies," I said cheerfully. Everybody stared at me as though I had the plague. "So we don't study. What do we do?"

"Hunt up boyfriends. Find ways to cut class without getting caught. Anything else that might be interesting," Karen explained patiently.

"You're bragging." Patty laughed. "You wouldn't dare."

"The boyfriend part is true enough, except you, Patty. You must be true to *lover Rollo.*"

"That is my fate." Patty sighed. A boyfriend! Patty! She seemed as nice as the other girls.

"You didn't tell me," I accused.

"Jeez, you never asked."

"Guess I'm from the country." They all laughed, but I felt my stomach turning again. Nothing I said was right.

"How come I've never seen Rollo?" I asked.

"You will," Patty promised. "His car is in the shop, so he couldn't make school today. Something to do with the valve lifters."

"He's missing school because of his car, and the first day at that?"

"The first day isn't anything. How can he get to school if his car won't run? Stands to reason. He'll be here tomorrow," Patty assured me. Apparently Rollo never heard of a bus or even hitching a ride.

"What's his real name?" I hated to ask the question for fear Rollo was an odd name, but my curiosity got the better of me.

"Byron Rollinson. He's a junior."

"And a weirdo," Sheena chimed in.

"Yeah, carries a screwdriver instead of a comb," Karen put in for good measure. I sneaked a peek at Patty, but she didn't feel bad. At least she smiled.

"He's a man, which is more than you have," Patty retorted.

"Don't you and Sheena have boyfriends?" I asked Karen.

"Thought we'd give the BMOCs a chance," Karen drawled. She knew I didn't have the slightest inkling about BMOC so she went right on. "BMOC is *Big Man on Campus,* my dear."

"There don't seem to be many," Sheena complained. "Feast your eyes on that guy over there." We all turned to stare at a boy who must have been well over six feet. He was all arms and legs. He wore horn-rimmed glasses, and his complexion was awful. I felt sorry for him.

Hastily I turned my back, but the others continued to eye him.

"You're right, Sheena," Karen groaned. "Most of these fellows would be good playmates for Charlie Brown. This hunt might make old hags of us."

I wondered if they would think Steve Hall a BMOC. I didn't ask. They would suspect I liked him. Why should I call their attention to what I considered the ultimate? It would just create competition.

After Karen and Sheena left, I turned to Patty. "Do I stick out like somebody from the country?" I whispered.

"You're fine," she laughed. "Lots of the kids will be wearing jeans. It's no big deal."

"You wouldn't fool me?" Patty was nice. She might have been trying to save my feelings, but I preferred being up front.

"Linn, all kinds of kids go to this school. It depends what you like. Do your own thing."

That was easy for Patty to say. The teachers saw it differently. It happened in art. It was such a thrill to be allowed in the class at all. I didn't want to be late, and there was only five minutes between classes. The key wouldn't work in my locker, and I was frantic. I tried it again and again. Finally it opened. I fairly threw my books in and took out a notebook, slammed the door and locked it. Hurrying down the hall, I knew it was late. I rushed for the door to the art room. I made it in time to collide with the teacher, who was walking to the front of the room with a collection of posters in his hands.

I watched in horror as the pictures went in every direction. I could feel my cheeks getting hot. I stared at the teacher helplessly.

"And who are you, my impetuous young friend?" he said with tolerant amusement.

"Linn Romney, sir," I stammered.

"You must be a sophomore. No one calls me *sir*. They call me a lot of things, but not that. Hosmer is my name. I hope you are a neater artist than it would appear at first meeting," he said, lowering his glasses and looking at me over the rims.

"Yes, sir, I mean Mr. Hosmer," I mumbled and quickly bent to retrieve the pictures. There was a real stack—I mean, wow, what a mess. I tried to keep them in order, and soon I noticed a boy's hand helping me. He surely had big feet. I glanced up. It was the tall guy with the horn-rimmed glasses. "Gee, thanks," I said, but I didn't stop gathering the pictures. Kids were coming in, and I didn't want them to step on any of them. I think now that I was the first student to class. The tall guy was talking to me.

"I know how you feel. I'm always knocking things over, tripping people, spilling things. See my feet," he said, "size 13 and still growing." I straightened up with my bundle of pictures and gently placed them on a table. I inspected his feet. For fun I thought I'd measure mine and walked over to place my foot by his.

"You aren't kidding!" I exclaimed. He shook his head solemnly. "Must be some use for big feet."

"To put in my mouth," he quipped. We both laughed. "I'm Rick Adams." Mr. Hosmer entirely ignored us as he attempted to put his pictures back in order.

"Linn Romney."

"I know. I heard you tell Hosmer. This class will be great. Hosmer's good. What medium do you like best?"

"Rick, I don't really know that much about it. I did some watercolors last year. My teacher said I showed promise, but that doesn't mean much."

"It must mean something, for you to get in this class. Should we sit down?"

"Why don't we sit in back? Stay out of trouble that way," I said. As I turned to lead the way to the back of the room, I almost ran over Steve Hall, who stood with his arms folded, watching. "Oh!" I could feel my cheeks getting hot again. "Hi, Steve," I choked out as soon as I recovered.

"Hi," he said quietly. He had a funny look on his face. I walked past and sat on the second stool from the back. Rick sat across the aisle from me, and Steve followed and sat in back of me. The room looked strange with its stools and drawing tables. I counted. Only twenty-two students in the class. There wasn't room for more. Cupboards lined one wall, and there were large sinks on the opposite wall.

"I'm going to be an illustrator," Rick said shyly. "How about you?" I shook my head as Mr. Hosmer went to the front of the class.

"I trust you students have now adjusted your drawing tables and stools so that we can dispense with the twirling."

My gosh. My stool was too low. I experimentally twirled around, and it did go up a notch. I kept going around and around because it was so low. It stopped. I jerked and twisted, but it wouldn't reverse. It was too high.

In the meantime the door opened. In walked Steve's darkhaired girlfriend. She hunted the room over until her eyes rested on him. Then she came to sit down opposite him. For nobody being allowed in the class, it seemed that everyone was there.

Mr. Hosmer instructed the students to come and get charcoal and art paper. I gave up on the stool and climbed down to get my supplies. Some climb. Mr. Hosmer wanted us to get used to the feel of the charcoal, and he asked us to work away while he talked. He told us we would be working with charcoal, the air brush, inks, watercolor and even oil. Our projects would demonstrate our proficiency. We would also furnish the illustrations for the *Pen*, the school literary magazine, the yearbook, programs and posters for the plays and operas and other assignments.

About this time I jerked the stool because I was a hunchback working at the board. Suddenly my arms were grasping air as I fell backward. I flailed for the girl's drawing table across the aisle as I went down with a crash. A burst of laughter punctuated my fall. As Rick dove off his stool to catch me, his stool went down with a crash, knocking into his drawing table. The table tipped crazily and went down, too. Mr. Hosmer calmly stood at the front of the room and observed the chaos.

"Look what she's done to my charcoal!" the dark-haired girl complained in aggrieved tones. I couldn't see because I was wedged between her stool and her table. She held it up. A black handprint scarred the left side of her paper. "You clumsy idiot."

I agreed wholeheartedly, but I was more concerned to get out of my predicament. Rick started to pull me out. I heard Steve's voice.

"Let me handle this. You get your things."

"Thanks," Rick muttered as he set his stool to rights.

The next thing I knew I was in Steve's arms, gazing into his blue eyes. In the movies we would have kissed, but of course we weren't in the movies.

"You have charcoal on your face," Steve said as he set me on my feet. I wanted to cry, but I bit my lip instead. Steve picked up my stool and spun it down a little. "Try that," he suggested. Perfect. I settled myself at the table, accompanied by a round of applause.

49

"Miss Romney," Mr. Hosmer said icily, "at this rate our class will be destroyed by the end of the term. Please exercise more caution."

"Yes sir—I mean Mr. Hosmer." Another laugh from the class. I turned to Rick. He wasn't laughing.

"Now, if we may proceed, Miss Romney?" The teacher waited expectantly. My throat was dry. I swallowed. My body felt like a sieve with a hundred holes bored through from staring eyes. After ages he went on to tell us that we had a chance to model if we liked. It would be counted as a project. He asked for volunteers. Steve raised his hand first, his girlfriend next. As others volunteered I thought about it. Best to model. At least I'd pass one assignment. I raised my hand.

"Ah, the dangerous Miss Romney has decided to oblige. Perhaps you could do an imitation of Miss Streisand in *What's Up, Doc?*" More laughs. "Class, I left a list of art supplies you'll need on the table near the door. Get one as you leave. Have the materials here next Monday."

Patty took forever to meet me after school. A load of books weighed me down. I shifted them from hip to hip. To take my mind off the edge of the book cutting into my hand, I counted girls in skirts. I counted those in jeans.

Patty didn't have a book. "Got to buy some paper," she said as we fell in step.

"Paper? Patty, you should see this list of art supplies I need. It would cost less to buy the store. Mom will have a stroke."

"Other students sometimes sell their supplies if they give up art. Don't know of anyone," she said as she waved at a girl. "Say, why all the books? It's only the first day."

I told it straight, even though it embarrassed the heck out of me. "Patty, my classes are too hard. None made sense except art, and believe me—that hour turned into pure disaster. I don't know what to do."

"Jeez, don't sweat it. Teachers never give homework to start out. Break 'em in easy, as they say. Tomorrow the work starts."

"Maybe you should tell my teachers. I don't understand. The words they use are about the same ones I use, but when it comes out of their mouths, it's another language."

"Nothing odd in world history and science. Give it time."

"Maybe I'm dumb." I fought down panic. Could the difference be so great? At home I got A's. Here I'd be lucky to pass.

"If your computer tapes were blank, you'd find out long before this. It's new. Bound to get easier after awhile," she said as we walked to the bus stop. I gasped as I saw Steve's girlfriend standing under a tree talking to the redhead from the park. She saw me at the same time and turned her back.

"Patty," I began slowly, "who's the girl over by the tree talking to the redhead?" I concentrated on the bus in case she turned.

"You mean Chari Miller, Steve Hall's girlfriend. She's talking to Kevin Pace. You don't know Steve, but you will. Can't miss him. He's gorgeous."

"We've met. He's my next-door neighbor's nephew, and he's in my art class."

"How would it be?" Patty moaned. "Not that it matters. Chari's had him sewn up for years. Oh, to switch places with her for a day!"

"What about Rollo?"

"Rollo is mine, but Steve is everyone's dream." Somehow I didn't like Patty saying that. The bus came, and I took a last look at Chari. It sounds crazy, but I felt a little sorry for her.

4

One thing I really missed from the farm was the food. I don't believe school lunch should be categorized as food. It tasted like steamed cardboard with rubber cement poured over to kill the taste. I washed mine down with clabbered milk. Patty and I ate together most of the time with Karen and Sheena, but this day we were alone. The school didn't need to worry about us asking for seconds or even lingering over the food. We ate what we could and scraped the rest into the garbage cans. We put our trays on the conveyor which went back to the kitchen where there was banging and the noise of dishes as the workers got ready for second-lunch students. I supposed their fate was the same as ours, or worse.

We were heading down the hall—which went on forever—when Patty saw Rollo at the other end.

"Linn, there's Rollo. Hey, Rollo, wait up." I didn't want to make Patty feel bad, but Rollo *was* weird. His hair hung down in his eyes, and he wore overalls. Nobody wore overalls except girls. I guessed he was so attached to mechanics he wouldn't give them up.

"Can't talk to you now," he called. "Got to get to auto mechanics." Patty waved, and Rollo turned to head toward his class.

"I doubt he'll ever realize you can't date a car."

"He could," Patty giggled.

"Guess you'll ask Rollo to the Girls' Dance?" I knew she would, but I asked anyway.

"Already did. I was scared somebody else might ask first."

"Never can tell how many girls are nuts over an auto specialist," I teased as we walked up the stairs to the second floor.

"Rollo's always bragging about girls falling all over him," Patty confided with a worried frown. "We'll be talking, and for no reason he brings up the name of some girl he knew months ago. He'll go on and on about how she said he had such neat brown eyes or how his muscles just thrilled her. It makes me feel like I'm not good enough for him."

"He must like you. Haven't you been going together for almost a year?"

"It'll be a year in February—Valentine's Day. We never really see a lot of each other. We go weeks without doing anything together."

"But he's there when you need him." How crazy this boy-girl business seemed, I thought. Here

Patty signed her life away to Rollo, and she was not even sure he liked her.

"Have you ever thought about playing the field? What could it hurt? Tell Rollo you want to date some of the other boys, too." I should have kept my mouth shut. I always say the wrong thing. I could tell Patty didn't like that at all.

"If you don't go with someone, then you'll be left out—sit home all the time." Patty turned to her locker and fiddled with the lock. It opened, and she got her books.

"Like me," I added.

"Sorry, didn't mean to hurt your feelings."

"Boys aren't the only attraction in life."

"Hey, come on. This is Patty you're talking to, not your mom. Don't put me on."

"I'm serious. The reason I came to Salt Lake was boys chasing after me. If I'm ever going back to the farm, I've got to prove boys aren't a problem. If I start dating, Grandma will never take me back."

"I don't know what kind of grandmother she is. . . ."

"The best," I inserted quickly. I was afraid Patty was going to say something about Grandma which would hurt our friendship.

"Then she knows that the only thing girls are interested in is boys. And that's a big problem. Girls worry themselves sick every day about what boys are thinking, and parents worry what the girls will do to catch the boys." Patty knew a lot about things. She made me feel like a baby when it came to boys.

"That's what Grandma said," I agreed reluctantly.

"Well, I'm starting to think she's pretty cool. She knows what she's talking about." Patty nodded her head wisely.

"But that means I'll never go back to the farm."

"Maybe it's just as well."

"Patty, you can't know. It's my home. I have a horse, and friends, and everything is beautiful, and there's Grandpa. It's hard to explain." I couldn't tell Patty how many times I cried, wanting to be at the farm. She made it sound as though I was becoming another person—kind of like Grandma tried to tell me. I didn't feel different. I was still me.

"So that brings us to the next question. Who are you asking to the dance? Don't tell me you aren't going."

"It's not that easy. Nobody's interested. I'm scared to ask a guy I know because he'll think I have a thing for him. Then I'll be signed up with someone I really don't want to date."

"You mean Rick."

"Wouldn't that give Sheena a laugh. He's pretty nice, but he's forever tripping over his feet. And tall—I'd be looking at his belt buckle all night."

"What do you care what Sheena thinks?"

"If I weren't so new . . ."

"That's an excuse. Ask Rick."

"He's been hinting," I admitted.

"Okay. So you ask him, and we'll double, or we can make it a big party and go with Karen and Sheena."

"Just double. I don't want anybody around when Rick takes a nose dive." I couldn't tell Patty, but I'd rather not have gone at all. I'd have died watching Steve with his arms around Chari. It was bad enough having to draw Steve in art class day after day. Even with all his mountain-climbing clothes, his muscles stood out, and I felt positively weird drawing any part of him. He had two days left to model, and I couldn't even get started.

"All right. We'll double, but you better be asking Rick," Patty warned.

"I will. I will," I said, but I knew it wouldn't be today. I needed time.

"I'll be seeing you after school, and you better ask," Patty said with a toss of her head as she rushed to her music class. I turned slowly toward English.

Later, in art, I lifted my sketch from the rack. It was big. It must have been at least two feet by three feet, and all Steve Hall. Not a smudge on it. That's because there were barely any marks—only a faint outline.

I moved to my table and got out the charcoal. Maybe it would be easier from memory. It wasn't. I sketched over the outline once again. I recalled Steve's bulky shoulders and his rounded arms. My fingers shook, and I set the charcoal down.

"Boy, I'd say Hall doesn't inspire you one bit," Rick observed from over my shoulder.

The urge to put my arms over the sketch to hide it almost overpowered me, but I played it casual. "Guess it's my farm instincts. I like a real man," I bragged with a tinge of hysteria in my voice. A prickly sensation between my shoulder blades urged me to turn around. Slowly I twisted on the stool. My cheeks burned as I gazed in horror at Steve, gathering his rope and pick and other paraphernalia from the side drawer of his table. "Oh, hi, Steve," I blurted out.

"Hi, little Miss Farmer," he returned quietly as he moved to the front of the class. A ladder was set up, and he climbed up and sat on the top, waiting for Hosmer.

I swallowed a couple of times trying to think of something to say to Steve. An apology wouldn't hurt. Grandma would insist on it, but not in front of Rick—later. I'd tell him . . . What could I tell him? That it gave me the jitters to draw him, that I was mooning over the sight of him every day and couldn't concentrate and that was the real reason I couldn't draw him, and—even worse—made fun of him? Best to keep quiet. I'd dig myself a hole and fall right in it.

"I'm having a hard time getting into this mountain-climbing thing, too," Rick complained. "It seems senseless to risk your life to climb to the top of a mountain. Once you get up what have you accomplished? You turn around and come back down. Now I ask you, would an intelligent person climb a mountain?"

"I think I would," I answered honestly. "I bet it's scary. But if you make it to the top, then you proved something to yourself."

"But if you're dead, what's to prove?"

"At least it would be trying."

"Why not try something useful—like painting—something others can enjoy. With painting you talk to people."

"So why couldn't you paint a mountain climber and tell people about the guts it takes to make it to the top?" I was becoming so enthusiastic about mountain climbing, I forgot all about Steve. I started to sketch.

I didn't even lift my head when Hosmer said, "Let's get to work. I'll begin checking the drawings today, that is, if any of you managed to capture the essence of our climber."

I knew that Steve moved down a couple of steps and stood with one foot on the step above the other as if climbing the mountain. The picture of him was etched into my brain, and my fingers flew over the paper.

Steve must have been exhausted with his arms stretched over his head. He rested one arm on the ladder, but the other reached to grasp an imaginary niche in a rock. I thought about the determination in his face and grew even more excited about my picture.

Concentration showed in the careful lines Rick drew when I glanced over. Then Rick's eyes lifted and I was surprised at the intent stare as he studied Steve and then turned his attention back to his drawing.

"You're really getting into it," I whispered.

"So are you."

"Yes, this is great. Look how much I've done already."

"Miss Romney, I'm sure the class is fascinated by

your progress, but may I ask that you continue to work quietly?"

"Sure." Me and my big mouth again. Always saying the wrong things. Slowly the mountain climber on paper came to life, and I teased and prodded him until he was clinging to a ledge, straining every muscle of his body to overcome the obstacle. My mind was floating; I added a few more touches as the bell rang. It felt right. Tomorrow I would finish. It would be a good reminder to hang in my room—not to tell me how lovesick I was over Steve, but to remind me how purpose and determination can overcome some pretty shaky problems.

I started to ask Steve to look at my drawing as he was putting away his equipment, but Chari was clinging to him like woolen underwear. Forget it.

"Can I walk you to your next class?" Rick asked. It sounded like a good idea. We had learned something together today.

"It'll give us a chance to talk," I answered with a big smile. I turned away from the sickening sight of Chari and Steve, but I couldn't shut out the sound of her voice.

"Stevie, poor baby. Let me rub your arm. One more day and it's over," she crooned, and I wanted to throw up. She went on. "Those muscles. No wonder you're on the weight team. I'll be glad when you don't have to model."

I'd heard enough. I wanted to yank her hair out by the roots, but I kept smiling at Rick and slipped my art paper into the rack. This time I was especially careful.

"That felt so good today," I told Rick. I tried to recapture the feeling as we walked down the hall.

"Sometimes it's good to talk things over, and then you get an idea," he agreed.

"I almost feel like becoming an artist. I'm pretty good at art, but not that good. I'll probably be a school teacher in art or science."

"Commercial art can use you. My dad owns an advertising agency, so I'll be set when I get out of high school. I'll bet he could use you, too. Wouldn't that be great?"

Look out, Linn, I warned myself. He was moving in. "You're not going to college then?"

"No sense in it. I've already got a job. What do you do after school? I mean evenings."

"I do a lot of studying," I lied. "I'm so far behind." That was for sure. "Those small-town schools aren't tough like East. I'm home at night, but that's where I have to stay." Until Grandma lets me come back, I thought to myself.

"Oh." I had done a pretty good job of calming him down. Now would have been the perfect time to ask him to the Girls' Dance, but then we'd have been right back where we started. It was Steve or nobody. I was only fooling myself. I'd end up asking Rick, but at least not that soon. It was rude to wait too long, but I couldn't bear to ask him at that moment.

"Been to the planetarium?"

"No."

"They have this quasar rock show with lots of crazy designs in fantastic colors. Like to go sometime?"

61

"Sounds great. After this report period." That didn't discourage him. He was closing in.

"You mean it? This might sound unbelievable, but I've never dated a girl before. I've never even asked. Always thought the answer would be *no*. Didn't even feel like trying. I never thought *you'd* go out with me."

"Rick, you're really nice. I feel at home sitting next to you in art class. I guess a date will be the same way, won't it?"

"Don't know. We'll have to try it." I felt ill inside every time I sneaked a glance at the happy glow on Rick's face. You'd have thought I'd agreed to give him a thousand dollars.

"This is my science class. Be seeing you."

"Tomorrow." Rick lifted his hand in a gesture of good-bye, and I swept to my seat near the window. I dropped my head in my hands. What had I done? My gosh, Rick was going to get hurt, and I'd have to do some fancy running. It wasn't as if I didn't like Rick. I did, but not to date, only as a friend. Wow, what a mess.

5

I hung my mountain climber on the wall in my room where I could look at him first thing in the morning and last thing at night. Every day I noticed something different, even though I drew him.

I kept telling myself not to get so wrapped up in Steve, but I couldn't help it. He was on my mind so much. Sometimes I thought he was a fairy tale which I used to make my life happy. Other times I watched him at school, and he was better than any dream. I was glad he sat behind me in art. Nothing would have gotten done for watching him.

He was taking notes on Hosmer's lecture. We were supposed to be relearning about art. It was the first time around for me, so I decided to go to the library that night to get more information. That Hosmer could think of the most work. I didn't mind, because I loved art.

63

The bell rang, and I stuffed my books and pencils in my tote bag. Art wasn't the same without Rick. I guessed he was sick that day.

"Linn, I need to talk to you." Steve's smooth voice sent a chill up my spine, and I stopped in my tracks. I'd waited over a month to talk to him, and the day had come. He usually said "hi" or "how's it going," but that was all.

"Sorry, Steve, I'm in a rush to get to my next class. How about after school?" My composure amazed me. I wouldn't be able to concentrate one minute in science for wondering what he had in mind.

"Right. See you out front." Even though I didn't watch, I knew he walked over to Chari and draped his arm around her shoulder. Heading out the door, I didn't look right or left.

My mind began clicking off ideas about why he would need to talk. Date? Get your feet back on the ground, Linn. Could be something to do with Dougie. Poor kid hadn't many friends. The two of us should take him to the park. Could it be Karlene? By the time science ended, I'd figured at least thirty-five reasons.

My locker was near the band room. Trombones slid up and down while clarinets squeaked and intermittent, loud blasts from trumpets caused a regular din every day. Guess it was their way of saying "school is out."

That day the racket was a haze, like sound when you swim underwater. I was thinking about Steve and how Grandma didn't want me to have a boyfriend. Okay. I chose Grandma. Now she should let me come back to the farm. I could feel Starlight's velvet nose against my cheek.

My head jerked up. The hall was almost empty. "Blast," I muttered. I'd done it again. Dreaming when I should have been getting my books. I tucked my books under my arm and hurried down the hall. It was hard to shut out the past. I heard a girl's voice call out; I waved but didn't look. Almost running out the front door, I searched out the bus stop. I wasn't late.

A gentle tug on my braid irritated me. I hate people to pull on my braid, and every once in a while some character does it. I whirled around to let the culprit have a taste of my temper. Steve's teasing grin took the starch out of my tirade in a hurry.

"Oh, it's you. Hi," I mumbled. Whenever he came around, I was more tongue-tied than ever.

"Don't act so excited to see me. For a minute I thought you were going to leave."

"Would it have mattered that much?"

"Usually when I set a time with a girl, she's there. But not you," he added.

"Disappointed?" I laughed. I was determined not to let him embarrass me, but he did it all the same.

"Just curious. It's not good for the football team to let one of us feel rejected. Might lose our next game."

"Forgive me, O Mighty Allah," I said as I bowed deeply and touched my forehead with my fingers and then gestured with my arm. I straightened and grinned. "Now, how do you feel?" I thought the whole thing ridiculous. He didn't care if I lived or died, and if he wasn't careful, Chari would get mad.

"Not good enough," Steve persisted.

"If you think I'm getting on my knees and kissing your feet, you're out of your mind." He measured me with half-closed eyes as he balanced his books casually on his hip. His self-assurance made me nervous. He appeared lazy, lounging on the school steps, but I knew this was deceptive. I had seen him explode into action on a football field.

"What I had in mind was a copy of your art notes for the next two days. We're going to stay in Brigham overnight, so I'll miss class."

"Chari will be there." Me and my mouth. Would she be there or with the team?

"I know, but I want the best. You take time with your classwork, and get all the details." Would he ever be disillusioned if he saw my grades in my other classes! "I don't want my grade going down."

There it was—the big reason. He needed my brain, not me. I shifted my books from one hip to the other. My throat choked up, and I came close to hating Steve right then, even more than when he'd been with Chari. I was tempted to tell him "no way." Lots of girls would have been honored to help out the exciting Steve Hall. There was no sense in fretting about it. I might as well have given him the notes.

"No trouble. I'm going to the library tonight to check a few things. You can have a copy of those, too."

"The class notes will be fine. I want them the day I get back so I can study."

"You're really Mr. Business," I said with a touch of sarcasm to let him know I wasn't frothing at the mouth for the privilege.

"Have to keep up when we're gone so much. I'm sure you'll see that I'm an expert in rhythm, massing, tension and what all."

"How can you be sure?"

"Because I'll give you a couple of bucks to copy the notes precisely as you write them," he answered as he dug into his jeans, "and because you're frustrated out of your mind that you can't have me." I gasped but he went right on. "And you're the best. You'll tell me everything I need to know. Too bad I can't return the favor."

"Yes, that is a pity," I snapped. "My education would expand beyond all expectation."

"If you only knew," he laughed.

I clenched my hands so I wouldn't sock him. My eyes widened as I saw my bus pull away from the corner. The usual cluster of kids was gone.

Steve's eyes followed mine, and he understood immediately.

"Want a ride home? Chari'll be here in a minute, and we can drop you off." I could just imagine. Chari could sit on his lap, and I'd sit in her usual empty seat.

"It's no big deal. I'm going with Patty." Did he really think I wanted to be the third wheel?

"You certain?"

"Do you think I'd walk if I could ride?" Steve studied me for a minute before he answered.

"Yes, I do." Then he changed the subject. "Ever undo your braid?" I saw his eyes stray to my hair, and I felt goose bumps all down my back where my braid touched.

"Every night," I answered, my eyes staring straight ahead to let him know he was being rude. "I have to brush it to keep it healthy, and some people say hair grows better if it's braided."

"Is that what you're doing?" he questioned. He reached over and took ahold of my braid and started twirling it through his fingers.

I jerked my braid out of his hands with a twist of my head, but he caught it again.

"It's too long already. I should get it cut. It's in the way."

"Say, you wouldn't cut it?" he protested. "You've never worn it long here at school. No one's had a chance to see it."

"If you had streams of hair caught in your pencil, draped in your food or hanging in your eyes, you might feel differently." All those things really happened to me, but I didn't care. I loved my hair. Sometimes I twirled in front of the mirror for the longest time watching it flare out.

"At least don't cut it until you wear it down once," Steve persisted as he continued to play with my braid. "Not very many people have hair that long. I never saw anyone—well, my grandmother had pretty long hair." His grandmother, of all people!

"I always wanted to be the old-fashioned type. If I'm going to be cool, I won't argue so much next time when Mom says we're getting it cut for sure."

"I didn't want to convince you to cut it."

"I know, but if I'm ever to grow up . . . or grow down, I better. Thanks for the hint."

He frowned and seemed about to comment, but something about my face caught his attention. After a minute he said, "Say, I notice you have freckles across your nose."

"Yes, thirteen. And did you also see my black eyelashes and brows? Most distinctive." His personal inspection grated on my nerves. For goodness sake, he might as well have been holding up a magnifying glass!

"You're right—thirteen."

"At least you don't need math help." I could have bitten my tongue. I hated it when I said such smart-aleck things.

"Trig is my best subject," he grinned. His icy blue eyes blotted out every sensible thought, but when he smiled my knees turned to water. I knew he could see the hungry longing in my eyes. "But don't forget the help in art. Say, I never did see your final drawing of me. Did it turn out like Scarecrow Sam?"

"I put my imagination to work, and it was tolerable. Hosmer gave me an A on it." I added the last in case he figured I never did get anything down on paper.

"Hope I can do as well by you. When are you going to model?"

"It isn't for another couple of weeks. I can't decide upon a character."

"Why not a farmer? You know all about it." His face was serious.

"Yes, I wouldn't even have to change clothes."
He looked at me kind of strangely and put his arm
around my shoulder.

"Miss Farmer, you wouldn't let that get under
your skin. Give big Steve a smile and tell him it's all
right."

He couldn't hurt me by calling me a farmer. I
loved the farm. At last I knew what he thought of
me—a little sister. Suddenly tears came to my eyes.
Before I could search in my bag for a handkerchief,
he flicked away a tear with his finger. I pulled
away.

"You didn't hurt my feelings. It's dumb me. I
miss the farm. I wish they'd take me back, and
sometimes the faucet turns on when least expected."

"Poor kid. You really want to go back."

"I love my grandparents, and I have a pony.
Gee, I don't know why I'm telling you all this."

"Linn, I for one don't want you to go. I'd miss
you." Sure, like he'd miss Dougie—only not as
much, I thought bitterly.

"Thanks. I'd miss you, too. I've got to get going,
or I'll never make it to the library."

"You be all right?" Steve held on to my shoulder, but I twisted away.

"Fine. See you when you get back from your
game. Hope you win."

"We will. With a running back like me, how
could we miss?"

"That's the great thing about you, Steve, all
modesty." I laughed as I walked down the steps.
Depression hung over me as I scuffed along toward

the bus stop. I hadn't gone far when I heard a voice calling Steve.

"Steve! Steve!" My eyes were drawn like magnets to the slim figure running toward the tall athlete. Steve paused to wait. It was Chari. Her hair drifted about her like a dark cloud. She resembled a model in her fresh, striped blouse unbuttoned into a low V with matching rust slacks. I couldn't help sighing a little. It was impossible not to overhear their conversation.

"You promised to wait at my locker," Chari said angrily.

"Did I?"

"You know very well at fifth period we agreed to meet there after school."

"Had to talk to someone," he said lightly.

"I'm sure. You deliberately tried to make me mad."

"No, I started following a girl, and the next thing you know, I'm outside and not at your locker."

"I don't think that's a bit funny."

"Couldn't help myself. She has this thick gold braid that hangs down her back, and it kind of bounces when she walks. I watched the braid swinging and bouncing, and here I am."

My hands shook, I was so mad. He was talking about me! How could he have made fun of me like that! I wished the ground would open up and swallow me in one gulp. I felt betrayed. So much for braiding my hair so it wouldn't attract attention! He wasn't serious, though. Making fun of me was more like it. Chari laughed, and my stomach turned over.

71

"Oh, you mean *Linn*. In that case I guess you're forgiven. We must let Linn have a little excitement in her dreary, bookworm world. But, Stevie, don't let it happen again."

His grin came to mind, and I turned in time to see Chari purse her lips meaningfully. I snapped my head back and stared at the ground in front of my feet. I didn't want to wait for the next bus. I'd walk.

I drew in a deep breath and watched white clouds drifting across the deep blue skyline to the west. I could see puffs of white smoke from the smelter out by the mountains.

"What are you dreaming about?" demanded a voice at my elbow.

"Hi, Patty. Rollo give you the slip again tonight?"

"Naw, his car is in the shop. Points need cleaning or something. I saw you walking and decided to tag along."

"And Rollo stays with the car. Every day he proves he loves that car more than you."

"I thought so, too, but he's proving different. He said I could take the bomb Friday to drag State. Want to come along?"

"I can't believe he'd let you use his car to chase other boys. You didn't tell him that."

"You're right. I told him I had a committee meeting for the dance, and I'd be late. Dad won't drive me so Rollo offered his car. If I happened to go by way of State, what could he say?"

"That you were chasing boys in his car and without a license."

"Linn, you're no fun. You think too much like my mother and not enough about fun," Patty complained. "How's your English coming, if we must be serious?"

"Sometimes I hate that Woody," I moaned.

"What's the latest?" She brushed back her feathered bangs for the tenth time. It was a habit. They weren't in her eyes.

"That research paper was our grade for the entire term," I protested as I lengthened my stride to avoid stepping on sidewalk cracks.

"I know that. We spent a lot of time on public utilities of our community," she mimicked with a sniff. "What public utilities have to do with English, I'll never know—and what an icky subject. Didn't she like your paper?"

"Hate would be closer. In fact, she wouldn't touch it with a yardstick. Said it was vile, or some such thing."

"Oh, Linn," Patty giggled.

"'Miss Romney,' she said." I made my voice as snooty as possible. "Have you ever noticed how she calls us Miss or Mister depending how ticked off she is? 'Miss Romney, this was obviously copied straight from the book, and where is your outline?'"

"Jeez, did you copy it?"

"Of course. You don't think I'd do research," I said with disdain.

"What will she do?" I thought Patty was more worried than I was.

"Woody the Witch says it's a C minus for me. I don't care. I never wanted to go to school here in the first place."

73

"At least it's passing," Patty said with a shake of her head.

"Let's not talk about school work. I'll develop a complex or something."

"We could use some help on the dance committee." Patty managed to turn the subject to her own advantage.

"I don't think I better," I stammered. Every committee member was expected to be at the dance, and I hadn't made up my mind to ask Rick. I figured I shouldn't go, not this year. It might spoil everything. Why did people ever think up dances? Only those with steadies would go anyway, and a few others who were brave enough to risk getting turned down.

"Listen"—Patty sounded pretty serious—"my room is filled to the ceiling with crepe paper to make those darned flowers. I need help."

"Okay." I relented. "I'll come over Saturday after dinner, but don't expect me to be on the committee."

"I don't expect a thing. Only, make lots of those fancy roses. Jeez, they said over two thousand of the things would be hanging around the gym."

"Girls fuss too much. Long dresses, taking the guys to dinner—it will cost a fortune."

"That's because it's only once a year. Lend a hand with the roses, and that will give you the courage to face the rest of the expense."

"You mean it will wear me down. Don't worry. I said I'll be there, and I will." Making the roses would be fun, and I looked forward to Saturday.

It was a long way home, but all downhill, so not

that bad. Dougie ran football formations in front of his house as I walked down the street, and he came running after me.

"Linn, come play. See my helmet and pads Steve bought."

"Wow, you a tough tackle?"

"Heck, no. I'm the quarterback." Dougie feinted back for a pass, but I had to discourage him.

"Sorry, Dougie. Not now. I've got to eat and then go to the library. We'll play soon. I promise."

"Shucks, you never have time anymore," Dougie said as he started back to his house.

"It's true, Dougie. Please, don't feel bad. See you." Dougie sat down on his steps and didn't say anything. I wished a whole flock of little kids lived on the street.

I checked the mailbox as usual on the way in the house. A letter, and from Grandma! All the heaviness I felt a moment before for Dougie flew from my mind as I opened the door with a whoop. I thought she had forgotten me. I tossed my book bag on the kitchen table and threw myself in the nearest chair. Addressed to me. Good thing, because Mom might get mad if I opened her mail, and I could never wait. I tore open the envelope and nearly ripped it apart getting the letter out. Two pages of neat, rounded letters covered both sides.

My eyes devoured every word. Grandma said she hadn't written because she wanted me to think about my own mom. She still loved me, and Grandpa sent his love.

Starlight's foal was growing into a filly, and she

loved to run around the pasture. Starlight always raced her and let her win. Grandma said they had decided to name the filly Twilight after all. Grandpa had been sick, but the doctor said it wasn't anything serious. They looked forward to seeing Mom and me at Christmas. That was all. She didn't say they wanted me back. Not a word about coming to stay. Going for Christmas would be wonderful, but not the same as staying.

Grandma didn't mention Mom writing. I knew she wrote. Maybe I missed something. I read the letter again and again. Mom found me reading it for the dozenth time when she came home.

"A letter from Grandma," I said before she could take off her coat.

"What does she say?" Mom went ahead hanging her coat in the hall closet and putting her purse away.

"Not much. Everything's fine. Grandpa has been a little sick, but he's okay."

"Can I read it?"

"Sure. Here." I handed the letter to Mom and watched her face as she read the letter.

"Sounds like your horses are kicking up their heels. Linn, about Christmas. I don't think we'll be going down." I could tell Mom had something on her mind. Grandma didn't ask me to stay, and now I couldn't even visit. The hurt never stopped when I left the farm, but now the disappointment ached so bad I wanted to cry.

"How come?" Talk about maturity. I thought lately I'd grown to be a hundred. Right then I should have been screaming and bawling.

"Linn, this might be tough for you to understand, but I like a guy at work a lot. His name is Joel. I really don't want to leave."

"A boyfriend," I supplied.

"Sort of."

"I can't go to Pepper Hill because you want to see your boyfriend. I guess he's more important than me."

"You always manage to put me in the wrong. Yes, you have to stay home because I want to be with my boyfriend. You're part of my family, so you'll stay with me." I could see another argument coming, but I hurt too much to hold back.

"I don't care if you don't go to Pepper Hill for Christmas. I'd rather you stay right here so I can be alone with Grandpa and Grandma. I'll go on the bus by myself. Who wants you anyway? You never cared about me for years. Never came to see me. Never called. Now you want to ruin my whole life for one of your boyfriends. I'm not going to do it. I'll earn the money and go on the bus and you can't stop me."

"I won't stop you." I couldn't believe she wasn't going to argue even a little about it.

"You mean it?"

"Yes." Something was wrong and I couldn't figure it out. Well, she'd said I could go. No sense worrying about that.

"I need to go to the library. Could we eat right away?"

"If you go downtown, I want you back early. I don't like your walking around at night by yourself."

"It'll be fine, Mom. Nothing has happened yet. Besides, I'll be home by nine." The bus didn't come our way, so I'd walk two blocks. A car would have been nice, but until we had one, I didn't mind walking. "Mom?"

"Yes?"

"Sorry I lost my temper."

"I know, Linn."

6

Bawling won't take the wrinkle out of Rollo's fender," Sheena pointed out as she gave one final twist to the pink, crepe-paper rose. She tossed the flower on the growing pile in the center of Patty's bedroom floor.

"He thinks I'm a complete idiot," Patty wailed from her Indian-style position on the rug as she tried vainly to wrap the paper on her wire.

"You're wrecking the paper with all those tears," Karen warned.

"I can't help it. He won't speak to me. I might not even have a date for the dance." With this last Patty broke down and cried. I hated to see her so upset, and I tried to think of the positive side. Although how backing into a pole at the drive-in could be anything but stupid, I didn't know.

"He should be grateful to you, Patty," I said reasonably.

"Grateful? You're crazy."

"But now he can spend more time working on the car, hammering out the fender. It'll probably take at least a week to get it smooth and re-painted."

"Linn, only you could think of that." It was a try, but Patty still carried on. "I don't even have a license, so he can't have the insurance pay for it."

"If you ask me, Rollo was pretty dumb letting you take his car. He should know you're too young," Sheena said, tossing another rose on the pile.

"But he taught me himself." Patty went into a new bout of weeping, and her rose crumpled from all the wet blotches.

"That only proves my point," Sheena said as she took another length of pink crepe paper and a wire.

"I don't care what any of you say," Patty maintained. "Rollo is wonderful, and he's so mad at me I can't stand it." She began a fresh round of weeping. I handed her the last tissue. The waste-basket overflowed. All evening we suffered the agony of defeat with her. She couldn't tell her parents what she'd done last night, or they'd ground her for sure. From what Patty said, they were understanding, but they had their limits. She'd be out of circulation the rest of the year.

I guessed Rollo was the only one who could make her feel better, but he'd never call. That character had axle grease for brains. Patty could call him and apologize again. No, she'd already done that fifty times over when she told him about the fender. I thought maybe I could call him, and he'd listen to me. Fat chance, but it was worth a try.

"Hey, Patty, can I use your phone?"

"It's in the den," she said. I shrugged my shoulders as she crumpled up her third rose in the last ten minutes.

"Patty, you're supposed to be in charge of these roses, but you're wrecking them faster than we can make them."

"I can't do anything right." She groaned. I hurried out before she started in again. Could losing a boyfriend really be that awful?

The den was two doors down. A lamp gave off soft light, and the cozy room with carpets and overstuffed furniture was a good atmosphere for a private call. As I sat down on the couch, I spotted Patty's *Leopard Directory* on the shelf under the end table. Byron Rollinson—easy as anything. I dialed. A boy answered.

"Hullo."

"Can I speak to Rollo?"

"This is him—I mean it's me." Great. Glad he figured it out. What Patty ever wanted with the jerk I didn't know, but if she insisted, I'd do my darnedest.

"Rollo, this is Linn, Linn Romney."

"Oh, hi, Linn. Whatcha doin' tonight?" He seemed friendly enough. I guessed Patty was making a big deal over nothing.

"Working on decorations for the Girls' Dance."

"Right. That's next week, isn't it?"

"Uh huh. That's what I'm calling about."

"Guess you heard about me and Patty being on the outs. Sure, I'd like going with you. Patty might not like it much, but after what she did to my car, I don't care what she thinks."

"That's not exactly what I meant, Rollo."

"I know. You're friends, but don't worry. It's all over between us." My gosh, Rollo really was taking the fender thing seriously. What kind of a creep was he? Patty was well rid of him, but she didn't think so.

"Rollo, don't you think you could talk to Patty and tell her that the fender isn't all that important? You two have been going together a long time."

"No way. Besides, what do you want us to make up for if you and me are going to the dance?"

"Rollo, I called to get you and Patty to make up."

"Really glad you called, Linn. Always thought you had your eye on me. I guess that's why you made Patty your best friend. I knew she couldn't get a friend like you without a reason. Don't worry. I'll show you a good time at the dance. I never thought I'd tell you, but I like you, too. Going to the dance will be great—just great."

"Won't you talk to Patty, and tell her you're not mad about the fender?"

"The fender's not a problem."

"Good. I knew you'd see it my way."

"I'll have it fixed by the time we go to the dance. Don't want you in a shabby car. I'll polish up the old bazooka, and we'll whirl around this town."

Sheena had him pegged right when she said he didn't have any brains. What a flake!

"Rollo, promise me you'll talk to Patty."

"If that's what you want, but I can't see the sense of it. She'll be mad anyway when she finds out we're going to the dance."

"Rollo, we're not going to the dance. I want you to make up with Patty." My voice kept getting higher and higher. Could he really have been that dense, or was he trying to put me on?

"Okay. Okay. I'll tell Patty it's no sweat about the fender. What say we meet tomorrow after school and iron out the details for the dance?"

"Rollo!"

"I hear you. I'll talk to you tomorrow after I talk to Patty." I gave up. "See you, Linn, tomorrow. Zoom, zoom."

"Rollo, don't hang up. Rollo?" My gosh, that idiot thought I wanted to go to the dance with him! What would Patty say? Had I ever made a mess of things! His antics stunned me. I couldn't move for a long time. I stared at the phone. I heaved myself up from the couch and dragged back into Patty's bedroom.

All three girls were busily making the roses. The pile was almost a foot high. Patty looked pretty calm, so I hated to add to her troubles. I sat down and started a rose. It was awfully quiet for some reason. I wished the girls would say something. Nothing like jumping in when the water's freezing.

"Patty," I began, "you were right. Rollo's pretty mad."

"That's what I told you. How'd you find out?"

"I called him just now."

"You called Rollo?"

I closed my eyes, but the roof didn't crash in. "I wanted to ask him if he would make up with you. I was going to tell him how upset you were." I got sick to my stomach when I saw hope shining in Patty's face.

"What did he say? Is it okay? Will he go to the dance with me?"

"Well, I think he's going to tell you it doesn't matter about the car." I thought I'd get the good news out first before tackling the bad news.

"Thank heaven," Patty breathed.

"But he thinks he's going to the dance with me." I watched Patty's face turn white. She didn't cry or say anything.

"This is priceless!" Karen gurgled. I didn't think so. My best friend thought I was a traitor.

"But you're going with Rick. You asked him," Patty whispered.

"No, I haven't asked anybody yet." I sounded guilty even to myself.

"You're supposed to be my friend," she accused as she dropped her rose and stared at me.

"Honest, I didn't ask him. He jumped to conclusions when I called. I kept telling him, all I wanted was for the two of you to make up. He kept saying he'd take me to the dance."

"You stole Rollo right from under my nose."

I had to convince her. "Patty, believe me, I wouldn't *want* Rollo."

84

"Now he's not good enough for you."

"Patty, let's not talk about this anymore. You and Rollo can make up tomorrow, and everything will be fine."

"How can it be fine when he's going to the dance with you? Who will I ask—Rick? I don't even know him. That's going to be one fine double date."

"At least you two have some boys to fight over. I haven't even a possibility," Karen put in.

"We can't double if you think I'd steal your date, which I never would. Please, Patty, trust me until tomorrow." I could see it was no use. Patty was too hurt to listen. All she could think about was that dumb Rollo. "I think I'll be going. I've caused enough trouble for one night, and we won't get anything done this way."

"My mom won't be here for another hour, Linn. You can't go by yourself at this time of night," Sheena warned as she put aside her rose.

"It's too dangerous," Karen added, but she kept winding crepe paper as she perched on Patty's bed.

I waited, but Patty didn't say anything. I didn't blame her. I'd made a real mess of things.

"I've walked it lots of times. No problem."

"I still think you better wait for my mom. Linn, this is just a misunderstanding. Patty isn't going to hold this against you. Are you, Patty?" Sheena turned to Patty, who continued to stare at the rose she was wrapping too loosely.

"What do you want me to say? Have Rollo and welcome?"

"I'm going." I got my coat out of the front

closet, and Sheena followed me to the door. My insides get queasy when people are mad at me. All I can think is to get away.

"Linn, you can't go. It's too dangerous at this time of night. Sit in the living room and wait if you must, but don't go."

"Thanks, Sheena. I'm glad you understand, but I can't. Being around with Patty feeling I knifed her in the back, hurts too much. I hope she can straighten that pea-brain out tomorrow. At least he said he'd talk to her."

"You're a good friend, Linn. Too bad Patty can't see it right now." I always thought Sheena didn't give people a chance, but I'd changed my mind.

"She's too upset about Rollo. I'd be shook up if she made a date with my boyfriend." I opened the door and stepped into the night.

"Be careful." I know she was embarrassed to close the door behind me.

"Don't worry. I walk home from the library lots. I always make it." Then she slowly closed the door, and I stood alone on the porch.

I knew Mom would be furious when she found out I walked home. It must have been after eleven. I looked up and down the street, and things appeared the same. It had never bothered me before. Why should it make me nervous now? Because it was so late, that's why. In the daylight everything is friendly, but after dark sinister forms lurk in every shadow.

An occasional car passed, and I stepped back out of the light each time so that I wouldn't be seen.

Stupid, but I didn't want to attract attention. After a few cars I thought that no one cared if I walked down the street at eleven at night or at two in the afternoon, so I didn't pay attention to the cars. At Ninth I was waiting for the light, and a black car like Steve's drove by. I didn't look to see if it *was* Steve. I ran across the street and headed south. I ran past about two houses when a car screeched to a stop beside me. I didn't want to stare at a stranger, but I was pretty certain it would be Steve. It was.

He leaned over and rolled down the window on my side of the car.

"Get in," he growled. I didn't say much as I walked to the car and opened the door. I didn't get a chance to sit down before he was yelling at me. "You crazy kid! Don't you know better than to wander around the streets at night? If I were your dad, I'd spank the daylights out of you."

"You're not my dad, and if you're going to yell, I'll walk," I shouted back.

"You need someone to knock some sense into you! Don't try getting out because you're staying right here!" I didn't listen, and I started to open the door. He grabbed me and pulled me back as he slammed the door shut.

"I made it this far. It's only two more blocks," I yelled. I pushed and pounded on his chest, but he was too strong for me. "Let me go."

"Not until you settle down. Linn, stop it before I hurt you." His grip tightened on my shoulders, but I didn't care.

"You can't treat me like this, Steve Hall! You mind your own business!" I jabbed him in the ribs with my elbow, and he grunted.

"Now you're really asking for it!" I guess I hurt Steve because he pinned my arms so I couldn't move a muscle.

"Let me go!" I gasped. His grip tightened, and I yelped.

"Tell me you'll behave."

"I will. I will. Let me loose, you overgrown bear!" Steve didn't slacken his hold one bit. "Steve Hall, if you don't let me go right now, I'm going to scream!"

"You would," he muttered in disgust. He was right. I was getting ready, and I took a big breath. The next thing I knew Steve was kissing me. Not a little kiss, like some parents give you, but he was kissing me like in the movies. I was all confused and upset from my fight with Patty, and then feeling scared, and then Steve was yelling, and now he was kissing me, and the next thing I was kissing him back. At first he was so fierce that he scared me. After a while he kissed me softly and tasted my lips. He lifted his head and stared at me in the dark.

"You're lucky I didn't take a swing at you. Must you always be so stubborn? You make me mad."

"I know. I'm sorry." Steve still had his arms around me, but I didn't mind so much anymore.

"Linn, what are you doing out so late?"

"It's a big mix-up. I was over at Patty's working on decorations for the dance. Patty put a dent in Rollo's fender, and he got sore."

"Were you in the car?"

"No, that happened last night. Anyway, I called Rollo and asked him to make up with Patty, but he thought . . . he thought I wanted to make a date with him."

"Did you?"

"Not you, too," I said bitterly. "Patty's sure I stole her boyfriend. I didn't want to stick around for my ride, so I walked home."

"And Patty let you do it," Steve added grimly.

"It's not her fault. She's too upset with her own problems to worry about me."

"But you weren't." Steve's arms tightened on my shoulders.

"You're right, but I didn't care. Patty's my best friend. If she doesn't have faith in me, what's the use?" I guess I felt a little sorry for myself. Steve shook his head.

"Linn, one person counts, that's yourself. What anybody else thinks comes second. It's what *you* think. Don't you care what happens to you?" When he put it like that, I felt like a kid throwing a temper tantrum or something.

"Yes, sure I do. Pretty dumb, huh?"

"I'd say so. You won't ever do that again, will you?" Steve watched me intently in the dark.

"My mom said that same thing to me a while back when I left in the middle of an argument. I told her I couldn't help it. That was wrong. I need to be more mature about problems. I'm not going to run away. I'll stay and work them out."

"That's a relief. I better get you home," Steve said, but he didn't move to start the car. He didn't talk either. It felt good to have his arms around me, so I waited. "Linn?" he finally said.

"Yes?"

"There's something I've wanted to do for a long time." He talked kind of hesitatingly, as though he didn't really want to say it. I started getting goose bumps.

"What?" I croaked. He didn't answer right away.

"Can I undo your hair? I want to see what it looks like."

"It's too dark. You can't see anything here, and besides, it's no big deal."

"Please, Linn. Let me." It would be a hassle getting it braided back up. It goes kinky when it's braided. It wouldn't look that good. Before I could say no again, I could feel him tugging at my braid.

"Steve."

"Sh-sh-sh."

"Steve, not now." His arms were still around me, but I could feel him struggling with the beaded elastic at the bottom of the braid. I didn't think there was a chance he could undo it because it took me all kinds of time to get it in. Before I could get a grasp on things, he was fluffing my hair around my face.

"Oh, Steve."

"Sh-sh-sh."

I could feel his hands on either side of my face as he ran his fingers back through my hair.

"It's so long," he murmured. He shifted sideways and bent closer as he lifted my hair and let it cascade down over his arm.

"I've gotta get home," I whispered. "I have the notes from class for you. I can run in and get them," I said, to divert his attention from my hair.

"They'll keep until Monday." His voice sounded far away as his cheek brushed across my hair.

"Steve, take me home." I said it straight out. He sat for a minute and then patted my head, kind of like he does to Dougie. He started the engine, and I breathed a sigh of relief. I didn't know what scared me, but he acted pretty strange.

I jumped out of the car as soon as he pulled over to the curb. I hollered out, "Thanks," and hurried to the door. He waited until I stepped inside before he pulled away.

I had forgotten my elastic. Oh well, I had a whole set. Mom was curled up on the couch all taken up with a book. She glanced up.

"How did it go?" she started out and then stopped. "What happened?"

"It's okay. Nothing really. It's a long story," I said and started to my bedroom.

"Just a minute, young lady. What have you been up to?" Mom got off the couch and stood with her hands on her hips. "I want to know what's been going on." Mom walked over and stood in front of me. From the expression on her face, I'd committed the crime of the century.

"Nothing much, really." She didn't believe me. I saw it in her disapproving eyes.

"Who brought you home?" she demanded.

"Steve Hall."

"Where's Sheena's mom? Listen, if you're going to start this monkey business, you can forget going

91

to the dance. No running around with boys until all hours." I almost ran to my room and shouted that she never trusted me, but I remembered my promise to Steve.

"Can't we sit down, and I'll tell you what happened?" I pleaded.

"If you think you're going to talk me out of grounding you, don't bother to try!" Her expression was furious. She pointed to the couch, and I followed her finger in meek humility. My confidence oozed away.

"What a big mess at Patty's tonight! First Patty cried because Rollo hates her." I couldn't tell Mom about the dent in the fender because Patty shouldn't have been driving. "I called Rollo to get him to make up; dumb move on my part. The idiot assumed I wanted to ask him to the dance. He secretly likes me. Imagine—he accepted. Honest, I never even asked."

"I bet Patty loved that." Can you believe it? Mom understood.

"She took it badly, so I walked home. Steve happened to drive by and picked me up."

"That hardly explains your appearance." Mom looked skeptical.

"He has this thing about my hair. He always tells me to wear it down. On the way home he asked to unbraid it, and I let him. Crazy."

Mom tilted her head a little as her eyes studied my face. I felt so confused. I decided to tell everything I could.

"Well, he foamed at the mouth and yelled at me for being careless. Even threatened to hit me. We talked it out. By the time he dropped me off, he cooled down." Somehow I didn't want to tell Mom about the kiss—a strange kiss, a dreamy kiss. Scary.

"You're not telling me everything, young lady. I've been around. No fifteen-year-old is going to outsmart me. Steve hit the nail on the head about your walking. You asked for trouble."

"You don't have to tell me. I didn't use my head. At least nothing bad happened. I'm just upset about the mix-up with Patty and Rollo."

"You can forget about the dance or any dates. I'll cut that off right now." For a minute I thought the ultimate disaster hit, then I reconsidered.

"Thanks, Mom. Great idea. This lets me off the hook. I can tell Rollo and Patty I'm grounded. The perfect solution."

Mom tapped her fingers on the couch. "Since you're so pleased, Miss Smarty, I'll alter things a bit."

"Hey, I don't mind. Ground me. Lock me in my room."

"The punishment is—you *will* go to the dance," she said quietly.

"But I can't. You don't understand. Patty and Rollo . . ."

"I know." Mom dug in her heels.

"I can't date. It'll cause trouble, and Grandma won't take me back." That slipped out. Scared, I waited for a slap or to see if she was mad or hurt or didn't care. She didn't show anything.

"I hope you get a date," she sounded like a stranger, "because you're going to that dance.

You'll look pretty strange by yourself, so I suggest you ask somebody."

"You hate me," I whispered. "You'll ruin everything."

"Just get a date. Time for you to be in bed. I want to hear Monday what happens."

My shoulders drooped as I shuffled to bed. I could've asked Rick, but he'd get hurt and cause me more trouble. Parents.

7

A whole school day without talking to Patty was awful. I ate lunch with Sheena. She said Patty still hadn't made up with Rollo, so I guessed I'd be going it alone for another day. I told Sheena I had to go to the dance whether I liked it or not. I could tell that she thought Mom was weird. She didn't tell me to ask Rick.

It looked as though Patty wasn't going to take the bus so she wouldn't have to talk to me.

"Linn!"

"Hi, Sheena. You talk to Patty again?"

"No, but you'll never believe what's happened." Sheena was flustered.

"What is it? Don't make a big mystery out of it." Sheena's cheeks were bright pink from running.

"I thought maybe I'd missed you. Good thing you're still here."

"Sheena, spit it out."

"Chari has chicken pox."

"Shades of polka-dot bikinis! She'll be ghastly for the dance." Who could ever imagine the glamorous Chari having an undignified disease like chicken pox?

"That's it. She told Steve to go to the dance without her. Bighearted Chari thinks he won't go, or at least can't have fun without her. She'd better watch out."

"How'd you find this out? Steve didn't say a word when I gave him my class notes in art. In fact, he hardly said hello."

"You don't expect him to run up to every girl he meets with a sign saying *I'm available for the Girls' Dance.* Chari told one of her friends, and it spread like wildfire. Three different girls told me. It's all over the school. I'm surprised you haven't heard."

"Haven't been myself today. Thinking of Patty all the time."

"It's so close to the dance, I bet lots of girls are kicking themselves for asking someone else. Of course, he probably didn't say anything to you because he knows you're going with Rick. It's your perfect chance. Karen could ask if you don't, but she isn't here today."

I didn't listen any more. My mind kept saying over and over, *you're going to the dance with Steve.* I completely forgot to say good-bye to Sheena and headed for the stop. I tripped over a raised part of the sidewalk and caught myself. I warned myself to be more careful as I turned back to Sheena. She laughed and waved. Concentrating on my feet, I got in line for the bus. As usual I ran the two blocks from Ninth. The way I felt, I could've flown.

Then reality set in. I didn't have a formal, and I hadn't bought tickets yet. The tickets were no problem. I could swing it, but the formal. All Mom's stuff was too sophisticated. Then I thought Karlene Haight's daughters might have something left over but it would probably be too big.

Before I stopped at my house, I went to Karlene's. She was busily stirring chocolate cake. I dipped my finger in the bowl to test the batter.

"Delicious, as usual," I pronounced, licking my finger.

"You children keep out of the bowls. Speaking of children, did you see Dougie on your way here? He hasn't come home from school yet."

"Not a sign of him." Where could he have been? He usually played in the front yard, in the sandpile, or rode his bike.

"I guess he's gone to a friend's house. He's been complaining all week about not having friends." Karlene talked as she put the layer pans in the oven.

"I know. I let him down the other day, when I went to the library. We'll make it up this week."

"I appreciate you taking an interest in Dougie. Poor little tyke. Guess I should talk to George about moving out farther south where the young couples live. I hate to do it. My friends are here."

"Dougie has friends at school. Besides, I think he likes to be around adults."

"That's because he gets his own way. He's spoiled something terrible. If we move, I'll be leaving all my friends in the ward. I don't want to in the worst way."

"Speaking of nice people, I want to go to the Girls' Dance, but I don't have a dress. I thought you might have something from one of your daughters. I'm a worse plague than locusts, but you're such a help."

Karlene laughed and then looked thoughtful. "Neither of them wears a formal now they're married. In the garment bag in the back bedroom I kept a few dresses. Do you want to take a look?"

"Could I?" I didn't know what kind of dresses Karlene bought her girls. I feared they would be plain, or girlish, or ugly, or the wrong color, or out of style; but better than nothing.

Karlene took the bag out of the back of the closet, and she began sorting through dresses. I stared at each dress with disappointment, a little girl's dress, too pale, really the wrong kind of dress. I marveled that so many dresses could fit in the bag as Karlene pulled a last one out.

"Here we are. This should do it." I stared. A midnight blue velvet dress—at least on top. The skirt shimmered with silver ruffles. "The dress will set your hair off just right," she said with satisfaction.

Don't get excited, I told myself. It probably won't work out anyhow. It's probably the wrong size, full of moth holes. . . .

"Maybe the dress should be dry cleaned."

"I can run it over to Ninth right now," I cried enthusiastically.

"You better check on the cost," Karlene warned.

"I have a little money saved up." I held the dress up to me and gazed into the full-length mirror on the closet door. "It's beautiful, beautiful, beautiful," I sang out, twirling around the room.

"Careful, it won't be beautiful for long if you snag it."

"Oh, thank you a thousand times, Karlene." I laughed and gave her a big hug. "How simply perfect. Wait until Mom sees this! Oh, the dance is going to be far out!"

"Why don't you try it on? It might be a little loose in the waist, but, believe it or not, my girls were on the small side."

It wasn't long before Karlene had slipped the dress over my head, and I grinned from ear to ear. Little straps of velvet across the shoulders, cut-out short sleeves. Lacing down the front suggested a plunging neckline, saved by a silver insert. It fit perfectly. To be exact, it dragged the floor.

"Turn the hem up a couple of inches," Karlene panted as she bent to mark the skirt with pins.

"Your girls must be pretty tall. I'm five five."

"They're both about five eight," Karlene said, giving the skirt a tug here and there and then nodding approval. "Better than I hoped."

"Mom has fancy evening slippers I can wear. Oh, don't wake me from this dream."

"Let's get this dress off you, Sleeping Beauty, before it gets trampled," Karlene said with a little smile, and she pulled it back over my head.

On the way home I wondered what Mom would say. I stopped to search up and down the street for Dougie, and I called, but no sign of him. It's getting late, I thought uneasily. I hope he gets here soon.

My concern for Dougie faded in the excitement of showing Mom the dress. She'd started dinner, but she came into the living room and admired my switching to and fro.

"What a good friend Karlene is," Mom said.

"Can I take your silver slippers?" I gasped out as I took a turn about the living room, pretending to waltz to an imaginary orchestra.

"Yes, you can take the silver slippers. We'll put blue ribbons in your hair. You'll be stunning."

"I'm so excited," I exulted as I went to my room to hang up the dress. I heard the phone ring and rushed out expectantly.

"It's Patty," Mom said and held out the receiver. I took it gingerly.

"Hi, Patty," I said.

"I called to apologize." Patty got right to the point.

"Then you made up?"

"Kind of. At least Rollo said he's still taking me to the dance, and the dent wouldn't cost anything."

"Then it's all fixed."

"You're not mad at me?" Patty asked.

"Course not. You were upset; I knew things would work out. We can double for the dance, okay?"

"Did you ask Rick?"

"No, I'm going with Steve," I chortled.

"When did this happen?" Patty questioned with disbelief in her voice.

"Chari has chicken pox, of all the fatal diseases.

She said Steve could go to the dance without her."
I almost laughed from sheer happiness.

"I don't know, Linn. Steve makes me nervous.
He's such a big shot."

"He's nice, a little too serious maybe. You have
to talk to him. Get to know him. Karlene Haight
lent me a great dress, and my mom's going to let
me wear her evening slippers."

"Do you still want Rollo to drive?"

"I don't think we'll all fit in Steve's sports car." I
giggled.

"Somehow I can't picture Steve in a four-door.
Well, at least it's the best-running car in town,"
Patty said with pride.

"Should we fix a dinner at my house or take them
out after?"

"Let's take them out. We don't want any work.
We still have the rest of these decorations to finish
by Wednesday."

"I'll come over tonight and help out, but I have
to be home early. See you later, Patty." For once
life worked out perfectly—Patty and I making up,
and the unbelievable miracle of going with Steve to
the dance.

As we sat down to dinner, the phone rang. Mom
answered since she was nearest. "For you," she
said and handed me the receiver.

"Hello."

"Linn?"

"Yes."

"This is Steve."

"Hi, Steve."

"Listen, Linn, could you do me a favor?"

"You don't have to ask. I meant to call you after dinner. I'm sorry about Chari and her chicken pox, but I must admit I feel it works out great for me."

"Yeah, I talked to her last night, and she said she's covered. She's pretty brave about the whole thing. Said she'd be back to school next Monday. She won't be contagious Friday, but she won't be at her best."

"Poor girl. Thanks for thinking of me, Steve. We'll have a super time. I have a terrific dress, and we'll double with Patty and Rollo. By the way, they got their troubles all straightened out today, so things worked out all around. I'm so excited. I won't sleep at all tonight. I think I'll stay awake and stare at your picture—the mountain climber."

He probably thought me nuts to race on and on, but I couldn't help it. I'd wanted to go with him so badly for the past two months, and now it had happened.

"Linn, I really appreciate your asking me."

"That's okay, Steve. Thousands of girls would like the chance, and I hope you have a good time with me."

"That's just it. You're so excited, I hate to throw cold water on the works."

"You couldn't do that. I have been so high ever since Sheena told me you could go with someone else, my feet haven't touched the ground for three hours."

"Linn, you're acting like Rollo."

"What do you mean, like Rollo?" My voice died in my throat. "You're trying to tell me I'm making a fool of myself, thinking that you're going to the

102

dance with me, but you're really going with someone else."

"Karen got me out of bed at five thirty this
morning to ask. I said yes. Linn, I want you to
know there's no one I'd rather go with than
you."

"Pretty stupid of me to carry on like that—
pouring out my whole history and making you
think I've been lovesick over you all this time.
Hope you enjoyed your laugh."

"Linn, listen to me. You had every right to
expect I'd take you to the dance, but it didn't work
out that way."

"Don't try to save my feelings, Steve. I'm not a
child."

"Stop it."

"Why did you call?"

"Dougie. The crazy kid walked up to my house
to play space cadets. I've been trying to get
Karlene on the phone for the past hour, but her
line is busy."

"Dougie! He's still not home? My gosh, what
could he be thinking about?"

"Would you run over and tell Karlene I'll have
him home in a little while? I'll fix him dinner and
play video games with him."

"Sure. I'll do it right now, but you have a talk
with Dougie. Karlene's been worried out of her
mind."

"Yeah, some kids never know when to go
home." Steve laughed.

"I'll talk to you later," I snapped, and slammed
down the receiver.

"What happened?" Mom's forehead creased into a frown.

"Oh, Dougie went clear up to Steve's because he couldn't find any friends. Karlene promised to call if she needed me to help search if he didn't come home. I'm going to run over and tell her where he is. Seems she's been on the phone."

"Calling around to find Dougie, no doubt," Mom surmised. "But that's not all. Steve's not going to the dance with you."

"I don't want to talk about it," I said and pushed my chair back. I headed for the door before Mom could see the tears streaming down my face.

Karlene nearly collapsed with relief when I told her where Dougie was. She'd been on the verge of calling the police, but she and his teacher had checked all his school friends first. Now, she had to call all the people back and tell them Dougie was safe. I left her to the calling.

After dinner I walked to Patty's. It gave me a chance to cry without having anybody feel sorry for me. I guess that's what happens when a person gets too excited about something. The bubble bursts, and everything is disaster. By the time I arrived at Patty's I had stopped crying, and the worst was over.

Patty came to the door. She took one look at me, and I started crying again. She held open the door, and I followed her into the house and down the hall to her bedroom.

"Linn, I don't know what's your problem, but I don't think you should do these roses if you're

104

going to cry. I ruined about twenty the other night, and we don't have that much crepe paper left."

That did it. I laughed. Then I told her the whole big melodrama, and she laughed, too. The only problem—no happy ending for me.

"I'm not going to the dance, Patty, even if Mom says."

"Linn."

"I couldn't bear to face Steve. Art tomorrow will give me a heart attack."

"How about Rollo? Should he stay home? We're going to double, remember? You better ask Rick, or his feelings will be hurt. It's getting close to the dance."

"If we live through this dance, let's not go to another."

"Are you kidding? The Christmas dance will be even more fun than this one. Besides, the boys get to ask, and we'll see what happens then."

"I wonder if Rick has been nervously pacing the floor, wondering if I'll ever ask. I'll put him out of his misery tomorrow." With the horrors of the day somewhat resolved, Patty and I set to work and finished the rest of the roses. We didn't splotch one.

8

I waited until time for the bell to ring before walking into art class the next day. My mind bounced like a ball, leaping for any casual remark to toss Steve's way. Rick to face on top of it.

Hosmer remained his usual self. "Glad you could make it today, Miss Romney." With eyes down I shuffled to my drawing table. The class tittered. Survival might be rough. I hung on, my mind numb to Hosmer's searching glance.

"Class, today we'll review for the test, Thursday and Friday finish up any projects in the works and Monday we'll begin with Miss Romney as our model."

Oh no! Devastation. Not right after the dance! I shriveled and looked for a hole to crawl in. The thought of posing for almost an hour with darting glances and muffled tee-hees sapped my energy.

"You *will* be ready?" Hosmer glanced expectantly at me.

"Oh, sure." Easiest thing in the world to let others cut me to pieces with slicing stares, and die a little every minute with Steve's sober gaze.

"Then we'll plan on it. I recommend oils if you haven't already worked with them this term, students." Hosmer went on and on talking about the test. I couldn't think about it. After an eon he summed up. "I think that covers it for today. See you tomorrow on time." I thought he directed a last quelling glance at me, but maybe I was feeling paranoid.

Then I heard Steve whisper. "Linn."

I pretended not to hear and quickly turned to Rick. "Say Rick, could I talk to you for a minute?"

Rick smiled as though I had given him a present. "I'll walk you to your class."

I gathered up my things, and Rick unfolded from his table. He managed to get to the door without knocking into a table leg.

"I've been meaning to ask you to the Girls' Dance for several days, but I couldn't get up the nerve," I began. "I hope you won't think me rude for waiting so long. Would you go with me?" I could tell the answer from his eager expression.

"That's a worry off my mind," he said. "I never thought you'd ask!"

"I think we'll have a good time. Rollo's going to take his car, and we'd be doubling with Patty and him, if that's okay."

"Super. Do I need a tux?"

"No, just a sports coat is great. The girls are

wearing formals, though." Out of the corner of my eye I could see Steve standing in the doorway of the class watching us walk down the hall. Rick put his arm on my shoulder as we walked the rest of the way to science. I could feel my face get hot, and I wanted to shrug his hand away; I endured to the end of the hall. My next thought really scared me. Suppose Rick wanted to kiss me good-night?

At first the shock of it hit me, and I couldn't think. Common sense came to my rescue. What's a kiss? No big deal. Unless Steve kissed me, of course. That would be another story. . . .

The night of the dance Mom didn't say much. She got off work early to help me fix my hair. We decided to leave it in a braid. She wound a coronet on top of my head with a dark blue ribbon laced in and out. She cut the sides a little by my ears for fluffy curls.

I had decided not to dry clean the dress but hemming and re-pressing it took forever. I kept testing the iron. It would have been like me to burn a hole in the skirt. When I finally slipped the dress on in front of Mom's door mirror, I grinned. Perfect. I strutted back and forth in Mom's spiked sandals, proud at not a wobble.

Would Rollo and Patty ever get there? I paced the living room again. Would Rollo be uneasy with me? I knew the feeling. I decided to put myself out to be nice to him. We managed.

"Hi, Linn," he said quietly.

"Hi, Rollo. You look great tonight." And he did. He had combed the hair out of his eyes. A light blue sports jacket, with dark blue pants, improved him a thousand times. Maybe he wasn't so weird after all.

"So do you," he said, helping me on with Mom's evening jacket. Slinky, but I'd freeze outside the car. After Patty and I exchanged *hi's,* my tongue stuck in my mouth. The silence stretched on and on. A couple of times Patty started to say something and left off. Rollo switched on the radio. The rock music blared. Rick lived on the other side of the world; we drove and drove. My hands started to get sticky. Relief poured over me when Rick hopped in the car—his happiness bubbled over and caught on. Soon we all laughed. Everyone talked at once.

At the dance Patty and I checked our coats as the music from the twenty-four-piece band excited us to get on the floor. The guys led the way into the gym. My eyes nearly dropped out to see the roses—thousands over the bandstand, on the basketball standards, strung around the walls. We threaded our way to the floor. A slow tune floated me toward Rick. I held up my arms. He enfolded me and bent his head toward me—no easy feat with him so darn tall. His contortionist act spoiled the effect, but he didn't seem to mind.

"Linn, I hate to tell you this," he began.

"Then don't."

"I'd better. I can't dance. The slow ones are fine, but I won't stand a chance at a rock number." I craned my head up at him and smiled.

"We'll get punch and cookies during the fast ones."

"That's what I like. Nothing fazes you. You always see the best."

"You make me sound like the Rock of Gibraltar."

"I didn't mean to." He sighed. We didn't talk anymore. Competing with the trumpets and trombones took all our energy, not to mention the crink in my neck and in Rick's back.

After the first set of dances we sat down, and Sheena and her date came over. He was medium height, had blond curly hair and was on the football team.

"Hi, Sheena. Can you imagine all these roses?"

"Somebody had better luck than we did. I'd like you to meet Jerry. He's teaching me a new version of the jerk."

"Hey, maybe you could teach me." Rick's eyes lit up.

"Sorry, old man. You're not quite my type." We all laughed.

"Linn," Sheena exclaimed, "those are some sexy sleeves on that dress. Where did you get it?"

"I forget," I said casually. That seemed to be the standard answer when girls didn't want you to copy their style. Suddenly I felt good. It would be a fun night. Lots of laughs if nothing else.

The music started again, and Jerry pulled Sheena to her feet.

"Come on, baby. Let's dance." The two moved onto the floor and then separated to gyrate to the music.

"If we watch a little, you could give it a try," I suggested, but I didn't think it would work that well. "Maybe if we went slow so you didn't get tangled up . . ."

"I've had nightmares about falling on my face. That's why I've never tried it," Rick admitted with a grin.

"I think the trick is to fake it. Just stand still and tap your feet. Don't try fancy steps. I'll dance around you, and no one will notice."

"You have a deal. Let's give it a try."

"Sure you don't want to watch a little more?" I suggested. It wasn't any use.

"What do you say we get out there and give it a shot!"

"Oh, Rick!" I laughed.

Well, we made an unusual couple, but we had fun. I had a hard time not laughing as Rick imitated my arm movements and swayed his body to the music. Once in a while he'd click his heels which gave the effect of dancing. At the end of the dance we were laughing so hard that we had to hold each other up.

"Let's give it another whirl. I'm beginning to like this." Rick smiled as the music struck up once more. As the evening wore on, we developed a more complicated routine. Each time we'd think of something new, we'd both crack up. Soon we'd be doing the new step with poise and confidence.

When we both got thirsty, we decided to join everyone at the table.

"Did you see the cute girl with Hall?" Jerry quizzed us. I didn't move, but Patty stretched around Rick to see. "Over by the big umbrella with all the roses." I turned. Karen was gorgeous with

111

her dark hair swept on top of her head and a few curls dangling at her shoulders. Her dress of frothy pink matched the flowers.

"She ought to be a knockout," Sheena muttered, "she was in the beauty parlor all day. Skipped school completely. Then she made her mom race all over town for the dress."

"It was worth it," Rick commented.

"They're coming over," Rollo said in surprise.

"Karen wouldn't double with us, so we're on our own," Sheena added.

"Well, come with us," I offered before thinking. I glanced at Patty, and she nodded.

"All right. We'll get some action tonight after all," Jerry promised. "I don't want to stand here chattering. Let's keep on the move."

Somehow politeness set in when Karen and Steve made it to the table. Karen drawled her hellos. Steve nodded to the guys. Everyone drank two glasses of punch, and Jerry and Sheena returned to the dance floor. Rollo and Patty joined them. That left four of us standing, eyeing each other.

"You two seem to be having a good time," Steve said.

"You bet," Rick answered. "Of course I'm not much with the fast dances. That Linn dances circles around me." I couldn't help smiling, and I tried to smother a laugh with my hand.

"Karen's a little tired. Rick, how about the two of you sitting one out, and Linn and I having a fast dance."

"Sure," Rick assented, a little too eagerly I thought. My eyes went to Karen's, because I knew what she thought about Rick. Either Steve didn't notice, or he didn't care, because he herded Karen and Rick over to some chairs and then came back for me.

Before he reached out to touch me, he stopped, and we stared. I didn't say anything. Then he led me onto the floor.

One advantage of going steady is learning all the latest dance steps. No question about it—Steve proved his expertise. I kept my eyes glued to him for cues. He had a way of dancing alone and then pulling me into his arms for a few steps. Each time he touched me, I melted. Let's go on forever, I thought. No laughing this time. Deadly serious, in fact.

As we finished the dance, he whirled me outside and guided me toward the chain-link barrier at the end of the dark hall. He tried a door, and it opened. Not saying a word, he pushed me inside and closed the door. We stood facing each other in the dark. The music seeped in ever so faintly. My heart caught in my throat.

"I don't know what you have in mind, Steve, but I don't think we should be here." I backed away as his fingers closed around my bare shoulders.

"You're so stubborn you won't talk to me."

"I can't see a need to talk."

"Are you going to let this dance end our friendship?"

"Of course not. I'll continue to say "hi" when I

113

see you, and you'll ask for my notes when you're out of town," I babbled. "I'll be happy to give them to you. Is there anything else?" Why didn't he stop talking to me. Going over and over my foolish mistake hurt.

"Are you going to continue being Miss Arctic?"

"You'll like her better than Miss Farmer."

"I don't. Please, Linn, let's be friends."

"What are you talking about? Of course we're friends. You sit right behind me in art. You're Karlene's nephew, and Dougie's friend. No problem."

"Sometimes I want to shake you."

I tried to close the image out of my mind of Steve in his tan sports jacket with a fine blue stripe which brought out his blue eyes. He wore dark trousers which emphasized his wavy black hair.

"Are you going to stare at my picture on the wall all night long?" he whispered.

"Oh, that. I was just teasing. I never could get the feel of that mountain-climbing business. Such a waste of time. I got a sketch of sorts, but Hosmer said I'd have to make it up." How could I say such awful things?

"I see." His voice was cold and his fingers tightened on my shoulders. I could feel his patience was wearing thin. "I'm not going to let you get away with this."

"You can't stop me."

"Linn, I thought you'd asked Rick to the dance long ago," Steve reasoned, but I didn't care. I wanted to get away.

"I would have, but one of my failings is leaving things to the last minute."

"I'm tired of your lies," Steve fumed.

"Then don't say anything. Let's go back to the dance. We aren't getting anywhere." I heard him suck in air, and I closed my eyes thinking he was going to lose his temper and shout at me.

"Are you going to let him kiss you?" So he'd thought of that, too.

"I don't know. Maybe. Sure. Why not?"

"I don't like it."

"And what possible business is it of yours?"

"None."

"Steve, you can't be my dad."

"I don't want to."

"Then stop all this. You're one boy out of four hundred at this school. If I want to go out with the rest and kiss every one of them, you don't have any say in it. You've been fun to know, but we're hardly close friends." Tears were starting to form, and I wanted to cry out for him to take me back, but I didn't.

Steve pulled me against his chest. I felt his arms wrap around me as his head bent next to mine. The spicy aroma of his after-shave did strange things to me. "At least you didn't wear your hair down," he murmured, and then released me. "Let's get back before they start looking." He held my hand and walked out into the hall.

It took a minute before my eyes adjusted to the light. Slowly we retraced our steps toward the blaring of the band. When we got in the gym, it was a slow song, and he pulled me into his arms. My forehead touched his chin as he held me close, circling the floor. When we reached Rick and Karen, the music stopped. We parted without a word.

Karen glared daggers as we walked toward them. I sat on the other side of Rick as Steve pulled Karen to her feet. He nodded, and they left.

"You didn't dance the slow dance," I said as we watched couples whirl.

"Karen didn't like the music. Seemed tired."

"Was she in a bad mood?"

"Heck, no. She laughed at my jokes. Hard to find an appreciative audience like her. Kept asking for more. Some dress she's wearing."

"Steve shouldn't have done that."

"Hey, it's okay. I'm not going to complain about getting stuck with the best-looking girl here."

"Thanks a lot," I said sourly.

"You're different, Linn. You're a friend." We smiled at each other then. As if reading each other's mind, we got up to wrestle through another dance.

Later, we went to Cummin's. It's an old place, but their food is tops. Kids jammed the place to the rafters. Laughing, talking and joking went back and forth between tables. Steve and Karen didn't come. I guess they went with his friends. The sick feeling in my stomach eased.

Time for heading home crept up before we were ready. We dropped Rick off first, and I walked him to his door. We smiled and shook hands. Rick's hands were huge but skinny.

116

"Trouble with going with others—no privacy," he complained with a laugh.

"You're right. See you Monday in art. Thanks for a fun evening."

"Hope we can do it again." Rick said politely. Rollo raced the engine.

"Ask me sometime," I called as I ran back to the car.

I guess the excitement of the dance had gotten to me, because I could hardly drag myself out of bed Saturday morning. When I glanced up at my mountain climber, I knew just how he felt. I staggered into the bathroom. A warm shower made me feel better, and I started on my list of Saturday chores. Mom worked the Saturday shift this week, so I'd be alone.

The kitchen was a sheer disaster. I tackled it first, humming some of the songs from the night before. Next, I interspersed vacuuming and dusting the living room with new dance steps I learned from Steve. I even polished the hardwood floors. My own room was a snap because I always kept it neat. Depression set in if it was messy. A light once-over for the bathroom with disinfectant and lime remover, then freedom.

I debated whether to go over to Karlene's. It would mean more chores and playing with Dougie. She might have an idea for my modeling assignment. I still didn't know what to be. Maybe a telephone operator, or a nurse. Karlene would have an answer, I thought as I pulled on my sweat shirt. October can be nippy.

117

I ran across the grass to the Haights' and up the front stairs. I rang the doorbell and had to wait. Dougie came to the door.

"Linn! Did you come to play with me?" he cried, all excited, which only made me feel guilty for ignoring him for so long.

"Sure, but I need to talk to your mom first."

"You spend too long talking to her. Let's play first."

"Who is it Dougie?" Karlene called from the kitchen.

"It's Linn, come to play with me."

"Come on in, Linn."

"Now, we'll never get to play," Dougie groaned as he shook his head and slowly led the way to the kitchen.

"Housecleaning the walls," Karlene explained when I walked in. "There's cleaner and a cloth right behind you." I picked up the rag and started on the nearest wall. It wasn't all that dirty. "How was the dance?"

"Lots of laughs," I answered with a grin. "Rick is so tall, we looked like Mutt and Jeff, but we managed. I even danced a couple of times with Steve. Is he ever a smooth dancer!"

"Yes, a little too smooth and too grown up for his years, if you ask me," Karlene observed. I wondered if Steve told her about my goof-up.

"He has a lot of confidence, but who wouldn't with all his assets," I said as I watched the cleaner roll down the wall before catching the drips.

"If you mean money, his dad is well off,"

118

Karlene admitted, "but he's had his rough times with no mom."

"I meant his athletic ability and his talent for drawing. I didn't know about his mom. What happened?"

"Caught in an avalanche up skiing. Let's see. Steve must have been about ten at the time. After that Harold and Steve went it alone. What a pair, those two."

"Guess that's what makes him so serious." I remembered our dance.

"He can laugh as much as the next person. I believe he's sensitive to others' feelings. I surely appreciated him playing with Dougie the other night." Karlene talked as she finished up one wall and began the panel under the cupboards.

"Linn came to play, Mom, not to work and talk with you."

"Now, Dougie, I told you I needed to talk, and then we'd play."

"Some problem, Linn?"

"Not really. I'm supposed to model in our art class. Kids do different characters or maybe just pose. Lots of the girls wear leotards. One fellow wore a Mexican sombrero and sarape, and Steve was a mountain climber. I have to model for five days, so I want it to be something interesting the kids will want to draw. Most of them will be using oils."

"You want to be pretty or ugly?"

"Be a witch," Dougie shouted.

"This isn't Halloween, although it's close," I

replied impatiently. "Unusual is what I wanted—a character."

"You could wear a little-girl dress and take a broken doll or something and look sad."

"Yes, that's better than a nurse or a school teacher. Maybe I should do something entirely different than girls would do—like a flagman with a reflector vest and hard hat."

"Now you're thinking," Karlene said.

"The teacher suggested that I portray Barbra Streisand in *What's Up, Doc?* because I'm always causing a disaster," I admitted.

"That wasn't kind. You see the movie?" By this time Dougie had given up and gone in to watch TV.

"No, before my time."

"Wherever that girl went, everything crashed. I mean everything. She wore a cap, red bandanna around her neck, an old brown suit jacket and jeans . . . and she had a back pack. She did have her more glamorous moments. One night she slept under the piano cover on the roof of an apartment building and had on a slinky negligée. Surely you've seen the movie on TV?"

"Nope. Both characters you describe sound possible, though."

"Your mom no doubt has something ultra you could use for the piano scene. Wear your hair falling down around your shoulders. You'd wow 'em."

"Karlene, I knew you'd think of something. What would I do without you?"

"Be a nurse," she said, matter-of-factly.

"I refuse to be a nurse," I said as I tossed the rag in the cleaning bucket and put the cleaner down. Karlene inspected the wall and nodded her approval.

"Come on, Dougie, time to play," I yelled. An Indian war-whoop answered. While I rinsed my rag and hung it to dry, I heard Dougie running from his bedroom to the front closet and back to his bedroom. "What'll it be today, partner—water pistols at fifty paces?" I didn't want to shoot water guns. Too cold.

"Football," Dougie announced with satisfaction as he appeared in the kitchen doorway with helmet, shoulder pads and a football tucked under his arm.

"Football it is," I agreed, rubbing my hands on a paper towel.

"Lunch in a half-hour," Karlene called after us.

"You hike the ball first," I instructed, "then go out for a pass and work your way back to the other side of your yard. I'll try to tackle you." We lined up facing toward my house, and Dougie began counting.

"Signals, 13, 25, 42, 91, 28, 60 . . ."

"It's cold out here. Hike the ball."

"Give me a chance. Now I have to start over. Girls." He bent back down with legs spread. "Signals, 24, 13, 12, 72, hike."

He threw the ball at me and I juggled it, but I didn't fumble. He ran out, and I threw a pass. I tried to make it pretty easy, but he dropped it. His crestfallen face made me feel bad.

"Have to do it over," I said and motioned for

121

him to bring the ball. It took three more attempts before we completed a pass. Dougie started back, and I went after him. I caught him on my ten-yard line. We both rolled on the grass, but he didn't seem disappointed.

"My turn to hike the ball," I said as I brushed off and stood up. Dougie was one big grin.

"Signals, 1, 2, 3, hike," I called out and handed him the ball. I ran a few steps and waited for him to throw it.

"Get out there," he yelled, and pointed to my yard. I ran out. He threw the ball. Could he ever throw for such a little kid! I caught it and started back. Dougie had no mercy. He came at me as fast as his legs could go and plowed into me. I sat down hard. Right then I noticed Steve standing on the sidewalk, watching.

"Steve, Steve, come play football. I creamed Linn."

"Way to go, pal." Steve patted Dougie on the shoulder pads.

"Why don't we take on Linn?" Dougie asked eagerly.

"No way," I objected.

"Sounds fair." Steve smiled. "First, I have to do something. I'll be right back."

"Everybody's always doing something before they can play," Dougie complained as Steve turned and walked toward my house. I didn't think much of it until he started up the steps.

I jumped up and ran after him. "That's my house. You can't go in there."

"Who's to stop me?" he called back.

"Me," I screamed and ran, but he already opened the screen door and tried the inside door. By the time I got to the steps he disappeared inside.

"Steve Hall, you come out of my house this instant," I shouted as I yanked open the screen door behind him. When I caught up he stood in my bedroom, just inside the door, studying my mountain climber.

I panted from running so fast, and I stopped short in the hallway. I watched his face as he scanned the picture. I couldn't tell what he thought. Now he knew I'd lied to him for sure.

"Satisfied?" I gasped out after a few seconds.

"If I were you, I'd have a talk with Hosmer. It's worth a C at least," he said quietly.

"You know darn well I got an A on it," I burst out, stung with indignation.

"Somewhere I got the idea you didn't get credit." He turned to stare at me with those slicing blue eyes. The staring contest might have gone on indefinitely, but Dougie banged into the house.

"Anybody going to play football with me?" he asked forlornly. "Linn, I'll let you be on my team," he added. He realized how pitiful my chances were against the two of them, a huge concession for him.

"Okay, but you run with the ball," I stipulated.

"Course, I can run faster than any girl."

I thought Steve would give us a gentle game. He wore loafers which would slip on the grass. Grass stains could ruin his jeans and sweater.

How could I be so wrong? I no sooner hiked the ball than Steve decked me, and then he went after Dougie. I screamed for Dougie to run, but the inevitable happened. The poor little kid fought gamely as he tried to bulldoze past Steve. Steve upended him for his efforts.

No way would we take this lying down. I jerked my thumb at Dougie to come back. "We need a conference," I said in exasperation.

"Huddle," Dougie corrected as he placed the football on the fifty-yard line (imaginary, of course) and walked over and bent down with his hands on his knees. I glanced at Steve who stood with one hand on his hip, smiling with self-assurance. I bent down, too.

"I'll hike the ball," I whispered. "Steve will tackle me, but I'll get up and run for the goal line. You pass me the ball. Don't let Steve near you, or you'll never get the pass off." Dougie clapped his hands and jumped toward the ball. I shrugged my shoulders as I saw Steve trying not to laugh.

"Signals, 1, 2, 3, hike," I called, and once again Steve flattened me. This time I tasted grass. Anger surged through me when I scrambled up and ran for the goal. Dougie weaved back and forth trying to avoid Steve, and I weaved opposite to make throwing easier. Finally, Dougie got the pass off. Miraculously, I caught it and ran in for the touchdown. My victory dance rivaled any you see on TV. Dougie screamed and jumped up and down. I gave him "five" when he could calm down enough to stick out his hand.

"It's only fair you hike the ball for me," Steve pointed out. "I'm a man short. As soon as I get the ball, it's open season."

"Sure," I said, trying not to show how it bothered me. I bent over the ball. "Signals, 1, 2, 3, hike." I tossed the ball and in the same motion turned and made a dive for Steve. I caught him around the waist, and he dragged me across the grass. "His ankles," I screamed. "Get his ankles." Like the warrior he is, Dougie piled right in there at the ankles. Steve fell over the goal line for a touchdown.

"Lunch," Karlene called. Believe me, I welcomed the reprieve. I brushed the grass off and headed toward my house.

"Aren't you staying, Linn?" Dougie asked.

"I'm going to the showers, kid," I said with thumbs up. Dougie trudged jauntily toward his steps, but Steve stood and glared.

"See you, Steve," I muttered, and ran for the house.

Mom got in after six. She sat right down on the couch and kicked off her shoes.

"Tell me dinner is ready," she moaned as she closed her eyes and lay back against the cushions.

"Dinner is ready," I announced with a little smile.

"Really? What did you fix?"

"This might not dazzle you, but it's hamburger with sour cream, broccoli with cauliflower and tossed salad."

"Sounds divine. Lead me to it." Mom sighed as she slowly moved off the couch and walked into the kitchen.

"Linn, what an attractive table you set," she said in surprise. "I'll wash up and be right in."

Somehow she didn't seem quite so tired when we sat down at the table. I said grace. At the farm we always said it, but I think Mom got out of the habit, living alone.

For some reason dinner seemed better than usual. For once Mom and I talked about our day. I left the part about modeling until last. I didn't know what she'd think.

"Monday I'm supposed to model in art class," I began.

"That's nice," Mom answered as she helped herself to more hamburger.

"I need to dress up. The teacher mentioned doing Barbra Streisand in *What's Up, Doc?*"

"Funny movie."

"That's what Karlene said."

"Haven't you seen it?"

"No, and I guess most of the kids haven't, but I don't think that will matter."

"What did you plan to wear?" She started getting into it.

"I thought a negligée."

"A what?"

"There's a scene where she sleeps on a grand piano—under the piano cover."

"Yes, I know that scene."

"Karlene thought you might have something

slinky, and I could wear my hair down over my shoulders."

"As a matter of fact, you'd be perfect for the part. I have a black negligée, but you'd need something more than that." Mom screwed up her mouth as she thought. "I know. I have a black satin sheath you can wear under it. It will look like a nightgown, but be perfectly decent."

"You wouldn't kid me? You'll really let me wear it?" Whoever said moms were pure pain? I used to agree, but I was beginning to change my mind.

"I'll help you with some makeup, too." She smiled. "Better not curl your hair. We can wash it that morning and then you can wear it straight. After dinner why don't you try on the negligée and see if you like it?"

Better not get too psyched up. Things could go wrong. But as it turned out, the negligée fit perfectly and so did the sheath—both of us were surprised. Mom and I are built about the same—height and all. Even her shoes fit me. She had black satin slippers with a little ball of fur like a bunny's tail. When I got everything on, Mom said I looked over twenty! Wow!

9

Monday morning early—when I say *early* I mean five o'clock—Mom sat me on a stool in the kitchen to apply my makeup. My cheeks were already bright pink from the blow dryer. It took forever to dry my hair.

First, Mom dusted my face with a light powder and then began with creams, pencils, liners, glosses, shades and whatnot until I worried that I would rival any clown for thickness of grease-paint. She hummed as she worked. Without hesitating, she picked up different colors and objects. It reminded me of doing an oil painting in class. From time to time Mom would tilt my face and squint at me, then go back to work.

"We'll use the false lashes," she said, carefully twitching the bit of hair from the plastic case.

"Oh, Mom, the kids'll laugh," I protested, but closed my eyes in submission.

"Linn, your lashes are dark, but from a distance we won't get the right effect."

"Good grief, if it takes an artist to apply make-up, no wonder I've never attempted the feat."

"Don't worry. With practice you can get it down to an hour because you know exactly what's to be done." Mom laughed as she continued to daub my face. "Close," she murmured, and traced over my eyelid. I worried the whole time. Mom's glamorous, but still, I didn't want to look overdone. I'd be a laughing stock.

After a good hour she took the dish towel from around my shoulders and handed me her makeup mirror. The girl who stared back wasn't me, but wasn't a clown, either. In fact, I was beautiful. I jumped off the stool and ran to Mom's room to check it out in her full-length mirror. She followed behind and looked over my shoulder with a pleased smile.

"Not bad." She nodded.

"I'll say." I couldn't take my eyes off myself. I turned this direction and that, and then I walked away only to come back and have another peek.

Mom had to hurry to get ready for work, so I finished folding the negligée and sheath in tissue paper. I placed them in a box along with the slippers. I decided to take an old duster to wear on top when I wasn't modeling. An old gray blanket would serve for the piano cover.

As I tied my hair back at the neck with a bow and

put on my usual jeans and a blouse, I heard Mom call out. I hobbled into the hall. "You going?"

"Yes, have a good day. Hope the modeling lives up to your expectations."

"Thanks for your help, mom. You're terrific."

"At least for a few minutes. See you tonight."

At school I tried to ignore the whispers and comments about my makeup. I couldn't help but hear a girl whisper, "Have you seen Linn?" Maybe they thought I was going overboard. I couldn't put it on myself, so I'd suffer it through. Several boys stopped and eyed me up and down. I became nervous.

Patty contributed her bit at lunch.

"Linn, I can't believe it. You're a totally different person. What have you done?"

"Be quiet Patty. Kids are staring."

"I'd think so. You've had a face-lift or something." Patty's astonishment worried me even more.

"Not quite. A little makeup to enhance my beauty," I said with a flair. "Don't you wear it?"

"It never did a revamp job for me. Who taught you?" Patty began to inspect me so closely I turned my head.

"Mom applied it. I'm going to model in art today," I explained sheepishly.

"Even your fingernails are far out," Patty commented.

"They're not long enough, but I'm not wearing false fingernails."

"You don't seem to have qualms about false eyelashes."

"Mom said it's necessary. I trust her," I said as I wolfed down my sandwich.

"Wish I could be in art class today to see the reaction."

"They never say much. It's work time. We get graded on our interpretation of what we see, so nobody's criticizing."

"What else will you wear?"

"One of my mom's long dresses." Well, could I go through the whole thing about the negligée? I rationalized to myself. The sheath was a long dress. My reputation for honesty remained untarnished.

By the time fifth period came, I bordered on nervous collapse. Changing in the girls' lavatory, I breathed thanks for the duster. Now to summon the courage to take it off when the time came.

Mr. Hosmer took roll as I walked in. He glanced up and his eyes lifted in question.

"I thought the art table at the back of the room could be the grand piano, and this blanket would be the cover."

"You're going to stand on the piano?" he questioned.

"I'll be lying down—you know, Streisand in *What's Up, Doc?*—the scene where she sleeps under the piano cover," I stammered.

"Of course. A couple of you boys put the table in front. Let's stack some books under the legs to raise it up a bit. And the blanket, Miss Streisand," he said, taking it from my hands. Hosmer spread it over the top and folded it back at one corner. He still wasn't satisfied and crumpled it back a ways.

"That ought to do it." He stepped back to view

the results. "Your piano awaits." He made a sweeping gesture toward the table.

The table hit me near the neck, and I stared. Turning around I tried to catch Steve's eye, but he was all taken up with Chari. Rick stared straight at me, and I motioned with my head. He hurried to my side. I took off the duster and asked him to lift me on the table. His jaw dropped, and he stared.

"The table, Rick," I hissed.

"Yeah, sure." His big hands grasped me around the waist, and he set me on the table. Steady, Linn, I told myself, less than an hour to let everyone gawk at you. I stretched out and propped up on one elbow. Hosmer pulled some of my hair over my shoulders to drape down the front of me.

The teacher stood back and studied me from one side and then the other. He told me to move back a bit, and then he adjusted the blanket some more, and then he fixed my free arm. Exhaustion overcame me before the posing began. I trained my eyes away from Steve the whole hour.

When Hosmer said, "Time to clear up," my arm and hand tingled, and I thought my wrist was broken. Mr. Hosmer helped me down. I hurriedly slipped my duster over the negligée. I massaged my arm, but the prickles drove me nuts.

"Excellent costuming, Linn. I wish all our models were as imaginative," Hosmer said. I couldn't help staring. Believe it or not, it was the very first nice thing he'd ever said to me.

"Thank you, Mr. Hosmer." I smiled as I gathered up the blanket and folded it. The bell rang, and I glanced up in time to see Steve leaving with Chari. Rick beamed as he walked up to me after filing his art paper in the rack.

"I take back what I said at the dance." He grinned.

"What did you say?"

"That Karen was the best-looking girl. Man, you sure fooled us. Cripes, I never saw anything to compare to you. You ought to see my sketch. I wish I could take it home to work on it."

"Thanks, Rick. I worried lots over the assignment. It turned out better than I hoped."

"Worried! You're too much!"

"Don't get carried away, Rick." I laughed. "I have to change. I'm going to be late for sixth period."

"I'll drop by and tell him you'll be a minute late."

"Thanks." I hurried to the girls' room to make the change. I felt so relieved. I even laughed a little to myself. How could I have worried so much? Steve hadn't said anything, but no doubt he forgot his own name with Chari back at school again. Still, he had never ignored me completely before. Could he be mad because I walked off after our football game?

After school Rick stopped by my locker. The sliding trombones were out in force, so we had a shouting match.

"Can I walk you home?" he asked.

"You don't live anywhere near me," I reminded him as I slipped my books into my locker and carefully tucked the box with my costume under my arm. I didn't dare leave it over night for fear something would happen. The duster could stay.

"I want to talk to you," he explained as he shifted his weight from one foot to the other.

"So talk," I encouraged, locking the door. We strolled down the hall toward the front entrance.

"Linn, we talked before about going out. How about tonight?"

"I told you—when things slack off." Rick reminded me of a puppy dog that jumps up again and again, anxious for someone to stop and pet him.

"I don't want to wait," he said, and his voice cracked.

"Rick, you're getting excited over nothing. We see each other every day in class. What's the big hurry?"

His face worked back and forth as if he didn't know what to say. "To be perfectly honest, I don't think you'll have time for me after today. Every guy in school will be chasing you."

"How many are walking me to the door right now?" I laughed.

"Me. You wait and see. I'll be trampled in a stampede." He shoved his hands in his pockets, and his face looked positively morose.

"You have my word. I won't forget my friends. Besides, I'm not into dating."

"You like Hall, don't you?"

I gasped. His question had taken me by surprise. I didn't know what to answer. I couldn't lie. After a long silence I replied. "Yes," I managed.

"He likes you, too," Rick said.

"We're friends, but it's not like that."

"What if he asks you to go steady?"

"What if Santa Claus comes in July? Rick, you're making a big thing out of this. You're my friend. That's what counts." I did like Rick as a friend, though he didn't exactly start my bells ringing. "Why don't we go to the planetarium later this week—maybe Friday?" I suggested.

"You mean it?"

"Why not? It's the end of the report-card period. Anyway, I hear their music is fantastic. A friend of mine told me."

"Thanks, Linn. Friday night. You won't forget?"

"Believe it or not. You can write Ripley tonight."

"Guess I'll be getting home. Can't wait to draw you tomorrow. Get a good night's sleep so you don't have circles under your eyes." He grinned at me before pushing the door open and walking out.

I stood at the window watching him go down the walk and disappear around the corner. His jaunty stride had quickly covered the short distance. I rested my head against the cool window pane. I felt very tired.

Patty was waiting at the bus stop. She usually went home with Rollo. I was surprised to see her.

"Where's Rollo today? Working on his points again?"

"No, he said something came up. It didn't make sense to me. I think he's trying to give me the brush-off."

"He wouldn't drop you. The past year he's been

like glue. Some fellows don't appreciate what they have, but they always come back."

"Where did you get all this worldly wisdom? You've never dated, let alone gone steady," she reminded me as she leaned out to see if the bus was coming down the hill.

"Didn't he take you to the dance?"

"I twisted his arm and humiliated him a bit—begged and cried," she said in disgust.

"Wait until you talk to him again to see what happens. If it's serious, start worrying." Girls spend most of their time worrying what boys think. Patty had already told me, and I had found out fast. I wondered what boys thought about.

"How did modeling go?"

"I thought you'd never ask. The teacher said I used imagination in my costuming. I guess I'll get a good grade—thanks to my mom."

"It would be nice to be talented in art. I'm destined to be one of those monotone, color-by-number, never-even-write-a-letter people."

"Some say it's talent. Personally, I think plain hard work is the answer. If you want to do it, Patty, give it a try. You can be in there modeling if you want."

"I think I'll try something simpler, like beginning art or art appreciation."

We had finally switched our minds from our troubles, and in no time the bus slowly wound its way down the hill to the stop.

I couldn't resist stopping by the Haights' to brag a little to Karlene about my modeling. We sat in the kitchen and ate peach pie with cream poured over the top. She always had something scrumptious. Between bites I described the details of my day—the nervous prostration, the body aches, Hosmer's compliment, and Rick's excitement.

"Two great minds are bound to come up with a winner." Karlene patted us both on the back.

"I don't mind saying, I was scared half to death."

"Don't have much faith in me," Karlene chided, but she smiled.

"Mom's going to be pleased. It's the first time we ever did anything together without arguing. She spent a whole hour making me up."

"I knew she'd be good."

"Can you believe? Her clothes fit me perfectly."

Dougie must have heard voices because he came running in the kitchen from his bedroom.

"Linn!" I tensed because I knew what was coming next. "Can we play football? Steve showed me some new plays. What do you have all over your face? You look sick."

"Now, there's an honest opinion," I laughed. "Young man, I'll have you know that is makeup. I am glamorous and sophisticated."

"Yuk. Don't get near me with that stuff. What's the matter with your eyelashes?"

"They're false, if you must know."

"What's that?"

"Oh, hairs are put on a little strip of tape. The tape goes on the eyelid," I explained as Dougie peered at my eyes.

"Could you put some on me?" he asked, fascinated.

"Yes, but I don't think my mom would like it. This pair is her best. I think they're sable or mink."

"Mom, do you have false lashes I can wear?" Dougie questioned as he yanked on Karlene's arm and jumped up and down.

"Dougie, I never wear them." Karlene deflated him in a hurry.

"Ah, Mom."

"There might be a pair in the medicine chest one of your sisters left behind, but I doubt it." The lapse, admitting a possibility that false eyelashes might be in the house, was sufficient cause to work Dougie into a frenzy. He tugged Karlene out of her chair, which was no easy task considering her size.

He danced all around her as Karlene padded into the bathroom to make a search of the medicine chest, and I followed right behind.

"Don't get excited, honey. You'll be disappointed when I tell you they're not here." Karlene tried to shoo Dougie away, but he climbed up, down and underfoot.

"No, not here," Karlene muttered as she snapped a compact closed. I smiled at Dougie as he hung on every word. "Well, that's out." Dougie's face fell. "You can tell how many times I've cleaned this out in the past five years," she remarked, setting aside several bottles for the garbage. "Ah, here we are," she announced in triumph. The lashes were ragged, but Dougie wouldn't mind.

"Yay-yay," he shouted, pulling on Karlene's dress.

"Dougie, stop it this minute, or we won't do this

at all," she threatened. This calmed Dougie a little, but he skipped about her as we moved back into the kitchen. Karlene seated herself on the same chair, and Dougie fidgeted at her elbow.

"Hold still, or this will never work." Karlene's tone was the most severe I'd heard her use. "Close your eyes. I've never put the things on," she laughed, "so this ought to be something to see." She smoothed the lashes, and they were crooked. She tried again. Dougie opened his eyes and skipped a little more.

"I said, hold still," Karlene hissed, exasperated, and she clamped Dougie between her knees. "Now close." This time Dougie made a valiant effort to keep his eyes closed until Karlene told him to open. We watched him expectantly. He batted his lashes back and forth, and we laughed. He ran for the bathroom to admire himself in the mirror. At the same time he left, Steve walked in the front door.

"So here you are," he said with a frown.

"I came over to tell Karlene about my modeling." I really didn't have to explain, but I felt kind of like Dougie—excited inside. I wanted people to know the sensation I created.

"Yes, she told me about her smashing success," Karlene added.

"Sure enough, a smash," Steve said, and he didn't smile. An uneasy feeling crept over me. Dougie saved me from further comments as he dashed back.

"Steve, Steve, look at the hairs on my eyes."

"Sure have grown some long ones." Steve grinned at Dougie, at least.

"Watch what I can do," Dougie said as he squinted and then batted his lashes.

"Starting him out young, don't you think, Karlene?" he teased. It made me feel a lot easier to hear Steve joking. Whatever he was mad about, I wasn't sticking around to find out. I stood up to leave.

"I gotta get home. See you later, Steve."

Steve frowned. "I came to see you, Linn. I want to talk."

"Okay, I'll wait." I sat back down.

"I mean in private." Steve gave me one of his icy stares, and I glared right back.

"We don't have secrets from Karlene," I tossed out flippantly. I saw Karlene's eyes narrow as she tried to figure out the problem between us.

"Linn, I'm asking you nicely to come outside and talk."

"Steve, let's play football with Linn," Dougie suggested, completely forgetting his eyelashes.

"Not now, Dougie," Karlene said and wrapped her arms around him and drew him close to her.

"I prefer to talk here," I said, stubbornly holding to Karlene's presence as a lifeline.

"And I don't, so come on. Sorry for the scene, Karlene, but Linn never likes to talk about problems."

"That's unfair," I retorted. "I said several times I would talk, but you're the one who won't say what's on your mind."

"Linn, you mad at Steve?" Dougie asked in a scared voice. Now I'd done it. Dougie looked upset. Steve had me cornered.

"Course not. He's my good friend. To prove it, I'm going to walk outside and listen to what he has to say."

"And you're not going to yell at each other?" Dougie whispered.

"We try not to raise our voices, don't we Steve?" I smiled at him, daring him to deny it.

"I've had enough of your antics," he growled. "Come on." He took hold of my arm and led me none-too-gently out the door. He didn't stop until we were in front of my house. "Shall we go in or do you want it here?"

"Here is fine," I said with courage I didn't feel.

"The little get-up you wore in art today was indecent." I gasped. Now that he said it, I knew exactly why I worried all day. Down deep I knew Steve would hate the negligée. "Linn, I don't know why you did it. Don't expect me to draw you because I won't. And go wash that junk off your face."

"Is that all?" My voice trembled, and I hoped not to cry.

"Yes. No, it isn't," he burst out. "I hated your hair." A tear rolled down my cheek, and I turned my head so he wouldn't see.

"Now is that it?" I asked in a voice so low I didn't think he could hear.

"Yes." He turned and stalked to his car parked in front of my house. He jerked open the door and got in. The tires squealed when he pulled away from the curb. I watched until the car disappeared from sight.

You might have known, I went to my bedroom

and bawled for over an hour. I didn't even think about the makeup getting smeared. When I got up and went to the bathroom, what a sight! Smudges of eye makeup streaked my cheeks, and small rivulets washed away the foundation, giving a striped effect with a mud mixture on my eyelids in white and beige.

I peeled off the eyelashes and set them on a shelf. With cotton and cold cream I began removing the makeup. So much for my little adventure into the world of sophistication and glamor.

Before I finished, I heard the front door close. I cringed inside. Dinner wasn't even started. I tensed as Mom's footsteps came toward the bathroom.

"Linn? What's the meaning of this? Dinner isn't started, and the table isn't set. What have you been doing?" Mom opened the bathroom door enough to see me with the makeup half off and a pile of used cotton balls on the sink.

"Well, if this isn't something. I rolled out at four in the morning to help you with your modeling outfit, and you haven't the decency to put soup on for dinner. If you think I'll do it again, you're mistaken. Have you been preening in front of the mirror for the past two hours?" She didn't wait for an answer. "Wipe that off your face, young lady, and get dinner going."

My shoulders sagged as I cleaned off the last traces of makeup. I tossed the cotton balls into the garbage so she wouldn't think me sloppy on top of everything else.

I didn't talk at dinner, and Mom didn't either. It

was my turn to do dishes, so I hurried to clean up. Mom got a book and went in the living room. With Mom gone, I dawdled over the dishes. What to do about modeling the rest of the week plagued my mind. Talk to Karlene? She'd endured enough for one day. Mom wasn't in the mood to listen. I decided to call Patty. With my mind made up, the dishes sparkled in nothing flat.

The telephone rang so many times, I thought no one was home. Patty answered.

"Hi, Patty, it's me."

"Hi, Linn," she said dully.

"Don't sound so enthusiastic."

"It's not you," Patty said. "It's Rollo."

"What's the matter—more car problems?"

"He dropped me."

"He what?" Today should never have happened. I didn't read my horoscope, but it must've been awful.

"I said he dropped me."

"Oh, he'll be back tomorrow. You know Rollo. All he thinks about is the car. He needs you, Patty. He won't let you go."

"He did. Said he'd see me around." I could tell Patty was crying.

"Jeez. Did he say why?" Who's to know why boys did anything? They got hot about the least little thing—like a negligée.

"All this time we thought he worked on his car. Well, he didn't."

"Patty, Rollo's nuts about the car."

"I know, but Brenda somebody-or-other is in auto mechanics."

"Oh." I knew when I registered that our curriculum needed some revising. Smart girl, Brenda. Auto mechanics.

"What're you going to do?"

"Look for another boyfriend. What else?"

"Don't you think it's a little soon for that?"

"I'm not going gray pining away for Rollo. Boys are like bus stops. There's one on every corner. At least that's what my dad says." She sobbed.

"Patty, what can I say? I feel terrible. I don't think Rollo's coming back."

"I understand. I'll be all right in a couple of days. If I could think of something else. Mom says there's nothing like another boy to cure you of heartbreak."

"Especially after a whole year." Steve and I had never gone together and I had cried my eyes out. "Patty, if you really want a laugh, listen to this one. Steve came over and criticized me for wearing an indecent modeling costume. As an afterthought he mentioned that he hated my hair. So what do you think of that?"

"I'd say he doesn't feel any better about you than Rollo does about me."

"I'd say you're right. The thing is, I go back to art tomorrow. I don't know what to wear. Shall I keep on with the same outfit? The kids will hate me if I change. Steve will hate me if I don't. He does already. Mr. Hosmer said he liked my costume."

"It's no use trying, Linn. It's going to be bad. You can't make everybody happy, and you probably won't make anybody happy. Why not do what you want?"

"I don't know what I want. Boy, is Mom ever mad! She got up at four in the morning to help me get ready. Now, she doesn't want to help the rest of the week."

"You're getting it from every direction."

"Really. I don't want to put my troubles on you. I know you don't feel much like talking when Rollo split."

"No, I feel better when I talk to you. If I sit in my room, I think too much."

"I know the feeling well. Cry a lot, too."

"I think I'm cried out. I wonder what I'll do when I see him at school."

"Look the other way until you can stand the sight of him."

"Linn, you're a scream. I wish I could help you, too."

"I think you did. Patty, in my room there's a mountain climber who's using every muscle in his body to get up on a ledge so he can see the beautiful view. I think we should use a little more muscle."

"But it hurts."

"You're right. But I'm going to do it on my own. I'll see you, Patty."

"Good-bye, Linn."

10

Fifth period came all too soon. As usual I got stuck in home ec, and I barely had time to run to my locker before heading for art. I went straight to class because Mr. Hosmer might wonder. When I arrived, he had directed some boys to stack books under the table legs. He glanced up, and then his mouth turned to a frown.

"A little late, Miss Romney."

"Can I talk to you?" I whispered. He cocked his head questioningly before motioning for me to step out in the hall.

"Mr. Hosmer," I began as a starting place, not having prepared a speech, but reciting over and over different methods of letting him know I would not be modeling the same costume.

"I can only presume disaster struck once again, Miss Romney, and you intend to throw us into

146

confusion." His dry humor got to me sometimes, but in this case his joke fit. I wouldn't
argue.

"I couldn't have said it better myself, sir."

"I've told you about calling me that."

"I thought if I kept it formal, you might not lose
your temper."

"Have I ever been known to lose my temper?"
he said, spacing his words so I thought he might let
go any minute.

"No, but there's always a first, especially when a
student grieves you as much as I do."

"I believe my constitution is sufficient to with-
stand anything you can dish out," he said coldly.

"I want you to know that I accept full responsibility for the inconvenience. If you feel you must
lower my grade, I'll understand."

"The problem, Miss Romney," he persisted.

"I only want to point out that sometimes I don't
think straight."

"Miss Romney, come to the point."

"As you know, I modeled the piano scene yesterday."

"I am aware."

I tried to think of some way to get past the next
four days without ever having to face the assignment. Nothing came to mind, and the world didn't
end, so I went on. "Today I would like to model
from the same movie, depicting Miss Streisand in
her traveling clothes—jeans, coat and hat. A mon-
tage effect might be unusual."

"Do you intend to appear tomorrow in yet
another costume?" he asked with narrowed eyes.

"No, this should do it for the rest of the week," I assured him.

"I suppose it has occurred to you that the students will now be a day behind in their drawing."

"I'm sorry for that." I shifted from one foot to the other as Hosmer's black eyes bore right through me.

"Let's not stand here wasting more time." He walked back into the classroom. With a wave of his arm he had the students remove the books from beneath the table legs. He nodded for me to stand on the table.

I strapped on the back pack after removing Dougie's baseball hat (that was the closest thing I could find). One of mom's blazers fit fine, and my jeans were the usual. I did bring a carrot with the green top which I held in one hand as it rested on my hip.

Hosmer appeared fully recovered as he ordered me in my stance and how to hold my head. Then he turned to the class. "Class, may I have your attention. Miss Romney, in her own inimitable way, elected to change her costume." The class groaned. "I shall not call the move unexpected, for Miss Romney seems to delight in keeping us on our toes. You have my permission to switch from oils to another medium if you find the time too short; but I think if we move along, we'll be able to finish by Friday." Some of the kids muttered and complained, but Hosmer didn't say more to them. He walked to his desk and sat down. Adjusting his glasses, he started correcting papers.

With my head tilted up, I didn't encounter glares from the students. I wondered if Steve was drawing, or if he'd given up entirely.

The class dragged on and on, but I didn't get half so tired as the day before. At long last Hosmer announced time to clean up, and I jumped down from the table. A couple of students gave me the hairy eyeball as they passed by, but no one got really sore. Rick came up as I shrugged out of the back pack.

"If I listed the disappointments of my life, finding you modeling in jeans and a jacket would come number one," he moaned as he showed me his sketch. Yesterday's sketch was on one side, today's on the other.

"One of life's little trials," I said as I headed toward the door.

"Wait. I'll walk you to class." He went to the cupboard to file away the sketch.

I gritted my teeth when he put his hand on my shoulder as we walked down the hall.

"Cripes, Linn, what made you do a crazy thing like changing your costume?"

"Too tiring," I lied. "I have to get up at four in the morning to get made-up. Not worth it. Besides, Mom threw in the towel, too."

"That's a shame. Some of the girls at school would be happy to help out, I know," he said. "Come on. Think about it. It wouldn't hurt to change back. At least we'd have you one day in each costume. We'd be just as far ahead."

"I don't think so. Hosmer already thinks I'm scatterbrained. I kind of like the get-up I had on today," I said offhandedly, but inside I steamed. Rick didn't care about me or my feelings.

"But I can see you any day in jeans," he objected.

"So that should make it lots easier to draw," I reasoned as I squirmed out from under his hand and tried not to look as though I had pulled away.

"But much less interesting," he admitted as his arm fell to his side.

"Rick, it's all in the way you look at it. I don't see anything that neat about a lady lying on a piano. When you think of a girl who has been to all sorts of colleges, given up her family, traveled all over, that's interesting, especially when she managed to stay free of problems while things crashed all around her."

"Especially one who caused things to crash all around her," Rick corrected.

"However you like it."

"I like it with you in the negligée," he said.

"Your mountain climber turned out when you said it wouldn't. This could be the same. Give it a chance. In a painting the artist brings his own feeling to it."

"That's exactly what I did yesterday."

"Sorry, I guess my inspiration is limited." I gave up. He was hopeless. The more he talked, the more I understood why Steve was so mad. I had sneaked glances out of the corner of my eye all period long trying to see if Steve liked the change. Too much to expect. He and Chari had left right after class again.

Rick walked on to his woods class, and I turned

to walk into science, but I heard my name. As I whirled around, I saw Chari, of all people, running toward me.

"Hi, Chari," I said surprised. She looked mad.

"Listen, I'm tired of your games. I don't know what you're trying to do in art, but it won't work! Leave Steve alone and mind your own business! What kind of a little number do you plan for tomorrow to show off for him? Go back to the country where you belong. We don't want you. One word describes you—misfit."

"You're just mad because I like Steve." My hands clenched, and I wanted to hurt her feelings, but I couldn't think of anything to say. Finally, my courage came back, and I looked her right in the eyes. "Better watch out. I might decide to take him away from you."

"Don't try it. I'm not afraid of you, but you keep your hands off Steve, or you'll be sorry." With that Chari marched on down the hall. The bell rang. Late again.

Going home on the bus, Patty and I wallowed in gloom. Neither of us spoke. "Airhead" loved Brenda. Chari declared war. Rick frothed at the mouth, and iceman Steve had given me the deep freeze. My modeling outfit brought on the blahs, and I needed a shot of novocaine to get through my other classes. Best not to think about my classes. I might suffer a coronary.

The next day my third-period teacher handed me a note to go to the counseling office. When I arrived, Mom sat across from Mrs. Pettigrew, my counselor. She never listened to kids. She made her mind up about life, classes, how to act, what to say, the answer to every possible question right at the tip of her tongue, so I had never tried to talk to her. Mom being in her office could only mean trouble.

"Hi, Mom," I said uncertainly.

"Hello, Linn."

"Have a seat, Linn." Mrs. Pettigrew gave me a winning smile, and I slid into a chair. "I've called this conference because I'm concerned about you." Mrs. P. took off her glasses and held them out to one side as she gave me her indulgent look. "We do try to help each student to succeed," she explained to Mom. "Naturally some students don't fit the mold."

"What seems to be the problem?" Mom asked.

"I have on my desk three failing notices from Linn's teachers." Mrs. P. handed me three pink slips of paper. I didn't bother to read but tucked them in my book like a marker. I stared at the floor. "We realize Linn came from a small school, and perhaps the work wasn't so challenging. It's hard to say without more information. We do have other alternatives for slower students." Again that tight-lipped smile.

Mom still didn't comment.

"I thought as a first step, we'd have this meeting and give Linn an opportunity to voice her concerns or desires. Also, I wanted to know if Linn received any special help at her school in—let's see, where was that?" She put her glasses back on and studied the card in front of her. "Oh, yes. Pepper Hill. Never heard of it."

"It's a few miles this side of St. George," Mom explained.

"Do you know if Linn had special tutoring there?"

Mom shrugged.

"Heck, no," I bragged. "Always one of the smart ones, but then you know how dumb farmers are." Mom gasped, and the counselor cleared her throat and studied the papers some more.

"Mrs. Neever, this is a very unusual case," Mrs. Pettigrew went on. "Linn is taking our most difficult art class, and she is one of the finest artists in the school. Her science teacher gave an equally glowing report. Her performance in her other classes is questionable."

"Do you have anything to say, Linn?" Mom asked quietly. It would take hours to explain how much I hurt inside, and how school didn't matter in Salt Lake, and who cared anyway? I shook my head.

"Perhaps you could give Linn a little extra help in the evenings," Mrs. P. suggested to Mom with a smile. "I know as a mother you're very concerned about Linn and want the best for her."

Mom nodded again. I don't know whether it meant she would help or that she was concerned or that she heard what the counselor said. I think Mrs. P. was getting upset with both of us. Her voice became more businesslike.

"I've asked the teachers to report on her progress daily so that we know exactly how she's coming," Mrs. P. said. "If she continues to fail, we would like your permission to do some testing to see if Linn has some learning difficulties or perhaps some emotional problem which we could help work through."

"I prefer to wait a bit before we take more drastic measures. Let me know if things don't improve," Mom said and got up to leave. She walked to the door and stopped. "Do you mind if I talk to Linn a minute before she goes back to class?"

"You can use the lounge outside the counseling offices if you like," Mrs. P. said.

"That won't be necessary. It will only take a moment." Mom smiled.

"Here, Linn, I'll give you an excuse for third period." She dashed her name across a note. I took it without saying anything, not thanks or good-bye.

When we were outside the office, I waited for Mom to start in about the grades.

"You aren't happy with me, are you?" she asked. She could've blown me away. Of course I hadn't been very subtle about the whole thing—getting good grades in the classes which interested me and not trying in the others.

"It's all right." I fidgeted.

"Linn, I want you to stay."

"You want me?"

"Sometimes you make me mad, and I want to smack you, but you're my daughter and my family, and I love you. I think you should stay. I know you love your grandma and grandpa, but at least agree to try."

"I'm trying—some."

"Please try harder for yourself, if not for me." She sounded as though she didn't know what to do.

"I'm okay."

"Linn, you don't want failing grades. They'll follow you wherever you go."

I had never planned to fail. "I'll bring homework tonight," I promised.

"Thanks." Mom walked down the hall past the office and out the front door. Strange seeing Mom at school. I leaned against the wall near the counseling center, still watching where she'd stood but a few seconds before. She claimed to love me. Maybe so. We didn't know each other much. I had been so busy thinking about Grandpa and Grandma—and getting back to Pepper Hill. Jeez. Failing notices in three classes. Maybe my teachers would give incompletes. I brightened a little when I saw Steve. He walked toward the cafeteria.

"Hey, Steve. Wait for me. Steve!" I ran (which you're never supposed to do in the hall). "Steve, wait a minute." He turned and waited. Did he ever look cool! Gray dress pants with a light blue shirt and matching sweater.

"Hi, Linn." He didn't seem happy to see me. So, I couldn't expect him to fall all over himself. Oh well. Best to tell him what was on my mind.

"You never said anything about my modeling. I changed in case you didn't notice. So, what do you think?"

"Better," he grunted.

"And my hair was braided."

"Uh hum."

"Steve, what's wrong with you? Now you won't talk."

"See how it feels?"

"I'm trying. Really. How disappointing. I thought you'd be all excited. Do you know how much courage it took? Everybody was mad. At least you could say something. I did it for you."

"I hoped you did it for yourself."

What did he expect? I felt like Dougie begging for Steve to notice me. "Well, I didn't. Sorry I bothered you. See you later." I saw his eyes drop to my book as I gave him one last withering glare.

"Wait a minute."

"Yes?" I turned back, brimming with eagerness.

"What's this?" My eyes popped as Steve deliberately pulled the pink slips out of my book. My heart dropped into my shoes. My face burned when he opened them and carefully read each one. At last he refolded and handed them back. I swallowed. I could imagine his thoughts. *You poor little dope. Too stupid to pass English. Frankly, I like my girlfriends with a few brains.*

He frowned and sighed. "How come?" Old Pettigrew ought to take lessons from him.

"For the sixth time, you're not my dad. If I fail, I plan to do it on my own—very privately."

His bright blue eyes never left mine. "Need help?"

"No."

"Then what?" Definitely a note of anger edged his voice.

"Nothing."

"Linn, you can't fail three classes. You're bright."

"That's just the point." I laughed almost hysterically. "Takes someone pretty smart to act so dumb. I manage it every day. You saw the proof."

"So you think it's funny?"

"Obviously. Straight *A* becomes a bore. A few failing grades change the monotony and give me plenty to talk about, such as how Woody is plain chloroform. I can think of a dozen insults." Why didn't he go away before I started bawling?

"I'm sorry about the notices. Maybe you could do something, but with the term ending Friday, I don't think so. Hate us all, don't you?"

I wouldn't cry, I promised myself. "It looks that way," I said with dignity.

"Linn, let's go somewhere and talk. You're in trouble." He reached out and took my arm, but I pulled away.

"Thanks just the same, Steve. Not much to say now. As you said, it's a little late. Poor judgment and a loose-leaf full of incomplete assignments don't change overnight. See you around." I turned and ran down the hall. I could feel his eyes watching me, and I ran for the first stairway. I went to the second-floor girls' lav. Shutting myself in a cubicle, I let the tears come.

Pettigrew's tolerance and my mom's disappointment were bad, but Steve's helpfulness wrung the last bit of pride and stubbornness from my temper. His eyes and Mom's—they'd haunt me forever. I choked and sobbed, and bawled some more. Somebody came in. I didn't care. If they'd let me stay on the farm, all this would never have happened. But it did happen, and I'd better start growing up. I'd lost Steve's respect. It might kill me. What a ghastly predicament! I never had less than a B at home. At least I could try. At first not understanding assignments might have been an excuse for lagging behind, but what was my problem now? Better get to the studies so Mom wouldn't be ashamed of me, too.

That night, making up assignments kept me too busy to worry about the modeling. I didn't think about Steve either. I tried to focus on getting my work in before Friday—not much time to do a whole term's work. Surprisingly, when I actually did the assignments, they took less time than I had thought. I whipped out one after the other as I studied at the kitchen table. Mom didn't try to help. She read in the living room. Later, she went bowling. I could tell she felt guilty. She even asked if she needed to stay home.

Thursday I turned in all the past assignments for English and geometry. (They took all night.) Both teachers said I would be penalized for being late, but I didn't complain. History—a different story. The reading was overwhelming. I'd study for the test as best I could and not do the assignments. I hoped the next term I'd do better and average out a good grade at the semester.

I stayed up all night Thursday studying for tests.

Both Thursday and Friday Mom put a light touch of makeup on me so the strain wouldn't show in my modeling. At the end of Friday I drooped. I wanted to go home and die. Rick ran up to me on his way out of school.

"Linn. Don't forget about tonight. I'll pick you up at seven thirty. My dad's letting me take the car."

"Oh, yes, Rick. The planetarium. I'll be ready." I'd completely forgotten. I never mentioned it to Mom to get permission. What if she said I couldn't go? I'd have to tell her I couldn't hurt Rick's feelings.

I plodded down the hall thinking of my mountain climber. This week I'd climbed at least two mountains, with a third coming up. I felt an arm go around my shoulders, and my head jerked up. Steve.

"Come on. I'm taking you home."

Sharing a bucket seat with Chari didn't appeal to me at all. "No, I'm going on the bus."

"You're going with me. Don't argue."

Frankly, I didn't have the strength. Chari wasn't anywhere around. Steve helped me into his car, and I sank into the seat. I huddled down and stacked Z's before he even started the car.

"Poor kid." The last thing I heard. To be able to close my eyes for a few minutes. Simply heaven. Such pleasant dreams, too. I dreamed Steve pulled me in his arms and kissed my cheek and my jaw, and nipped at the lobe of my ear. I didn't ever want to wake up. I wanted him to kiss my lips, but he kissed my eyes and my brow and my cheek again, and then my neck. Would he ever kiss my lips? I held up my lips and strained toward him. Finally. I reached out to pull him close and kissed him again and again. The dream faded all too soon. I felt the car stop and I opened my eyes. Steve grinned at me.

"Thanks for the ride," I mumbled, looking around for my things. My purse lay on the floor along with my books. I picked them up as Steve got out of the car and went around to open my door. I kept my eyes on my shoes. I didn't want to look at his lips. If he only knew my dream! I hurried into the house. Now to convince Mom to let me go on a date.

"Linn, do you really think you deserve to go out on a date?" Mom questioned, the way I knew she would.

"No, but what can I say? I forgot about it. You'd have to know Rick to understand. He worried because he thought I'd date dozens of boys and so I gave in and told him Friday. Then I forgot. The problems with modeling and my grades knocked it out of my head. I don't dare call and say I can't go because he'll think I'm rejecting him."

Mom's arms were folded across her chest, and she stood and looked at me.

"Please, not for me, for Rick. I don't want to hurt him."

"I don't either," Mom agreed.

"Then I can go?"

"Yes, but don't stay out until all hours."

"No problem with Rick. He's a nice guy."

160

"I hope so. You're young to go on a single date, Linn."

"If it makes you feel better, it's sort of an art project. We're going to see the quasar designs at the planetarium."

"Some project." Mom laughed. "Be in early. You haven't had much sleep the past two nights."

"I will. Thanks, Mom." I gave her a hug—a self-conscious hug, but I'd never hugged my mom before.

11

Being so exhausted, I thought wearing jeans and loafers the very thing, but Rick would want me to look nice. With a sigh I pulled out a pink Sunday-go-to-meeting dress with puff sleeves, bows, dotted swiss inserts and a flared skirt. The outfit had seen little use the past couple of months. Linn, don't torture yourself with high heels, I told myself, but the more I thought about it, the more inevitable it became.

However, a shower picked me up, and I hummed while I rebraided my hair. By the time Rick arrived, my spirits had revived, and I managed a sincere smile.

"We could've asked Patty and Rollo to come along," he said as he backed out of the driveway over the curb. The car lurched and bounced, but I didn't crack a smile.

"No, they broke up Monday."

"No kidding?"

"Patty's taking it hard."

"Gee, that's tough." It surprised me that Rick offered to double. He'd insisted we go alone. "We'll have to find her another guy." I didn't answer. Rick didn't understand that boyfriends didn't come that easy.

Never had I been to the planetarium for a show. Rick pointed out the large reclining seats in the back as preferred seating so we could see the whole ceiling. I relaxed into the leather armchair and waited for the fireworks to begin until Rick reached over and took my hand. Oh well, holding hands. I was thankful the large chairs prevented any closer contact.

For the next hour all kinds of visual designs dazzled us. When we walked out, I could still see neon spots before my eyes.

"Name your favorite," Rick said eagerly.

"I think the cloud effect. At first I wasn't sure that was the idea until they became more definite. Exciting to see them change formations. How about you?"

"I liked the dots and blips chasing each other in and out of one design after another."

"Neat," I agreed. We could see little puffs of breath in the chilly night air as we ambled down the street toward the car. He still held my hand. My own fault. Boys and girls can't be friends, I decided. If you go to a movie or on a date, it's because you're personally interested. Rick couldn't be that kind of friend, and it made me nervous. He

opened the car door for me and helped me inside
—very polite. I became more uncomfortable by
the minute. I leaned over and pulled up the lock.

"Thanks," he said as he slid under the wheel.
"Would you like to go to Fernwood's?"

"It's too cold for ice cream. To tell the truth,
Rick, I'm kind of tired. The show was great, but I
belong at home."

"No way. We just started. Why, it can't be much
after eleven, if that. What about heading up to
Trolley Square and trying the disco?"

"I'm a little young. Don't you have to be eigh-
teen?"

"No problem," he assured me as he turned the
car toward Seventh. He should be a little more
careful on those left-hand turns, I thought, and the
right ones on a red light. We made it without an
accident, but a couple of times I told myself not to
cringe.

When we got inside the disco, only three couples
were dancing. One guy was doing some kind of
contortions. I thought he must be double-jointed;
he didn't even have a partner. Psychedelic lights,
stale smoke mixed with pizza and a steady hubbub
of voices enveloped us as we made our way to a
table. I couldn't see a soul until my eyes adjusted to
the lights. All the couples were sitting at tables. I
wondered why more of them didn't dance.

Spotlights flooded the dance floor, and one couple really had the hang of things. They did wrap-
arounds and layouts, and the girl did the splits.
They were really into it.

"Come on, Linn. Let's give our little routine a

go," Rick whispered. "These people better prepare for a shocker!"

"Rick, I'd rather go on home." My body ached for the girl who threw herself into her partner's arms for a spin. Watching sapped all my strength.

"Hey, I paid ten bucks for us to come in here. We can't leave now," he objected, pulling me out onto the floor. I danced. Home looked plenty good now. Somehow the hilarity of Rick's dancing fell flat at the disco. Never one to be self-conscious, I did my own thing, and Rick matched my movements. The music blared, and lights whirled before my eyes.

I lost track of time. One dance merged into the next. I hated begging to go home, so I kept quiet. The torture went on and on. My legs ached, and my feet hurt. My back solidified into a question-mark shape, but I danced and laughed.

People started to leave, and my eyes followed them all the way out the door. The hyped-up Rick might never find his way home! He thought of more steps to try. I staggered back to the floor. Squeezing a year's dates into one night destroyed me.

Between dances I had a ginger ale and Rick drank a root beer. He upended the glass. Two gulps and gone.

"Drink up," he urged. "We're missing that far-out music." His body jiggled to the beat of the music, and my eyes saw double Ricks. Oh, to rest my head on the table for a minute; then I'd dance again. I pushed the drink aside and headed for the dance floor. My eyes refused to stay open.

They never played a slow tune, and the colored lights flashed and went around and around. I didn't know reality when I saw it. A hazy fuzz fluffed over everything. I floated.

"Heck, it's time to go," Rick groaned dejectedly.

"What! Closing time? It must be one or two in the morning." I panicked enough to see straight. We got our coats and filed out with the rest of the dancers. "Rick, I better get home." Mom would have a fit!

"At least let's stop and get a hamburger," Rick pleaded. "I'm starved."

"I've got an idea. Take me home, and you get a hamburger."

"Hey, I know a lot of guys do that, but I'm not cheap. I'll get you something to eat. I'm not going to drop you off hungry."

"Drop me off *starving*. I want to go to bed."

"Listen, we'll go to the Arctic Circle on Ninth. They stay open late, and it won't take that long." How could I make him take me home?

We walked down the steps into the lower-level parking terrace. I didn't talk. My mind fuses blew, too weary to function. We ended up at the Arctic Circle—so much for my powers of persuasion!

The quick service turned out to be over a half-hour wait. I guessed that everyone else had had the same idea. I ran up the steps to my house more than an hour later after many discussions and much pleading. I didn't stop running until the door was locked behind me, and I shut out the porch light. I stood dazed for a few seconds before I realized Mom sat on the couch. Her grim face told me everything.

"A little late, Linn."

"What time is it?" I asked, dreading the answer.

"Three fifteen," Mom said, without any emotion whatever.

"My gosh," I moaned as I sank down on the couch beside her. "You worried out of your mind?"

"Yes."

"I'm sorry, so terribly sorry." I knew that didn't help. "Mom, I know this might sound stupid, but I couldn't get Rick to bring me home."

"Linn, if you can't keep your word, you can't date," she said.

"You're right," I agreed.

"Want to tell me what happened?"

"Sure. We went to the planetarium and afterward Rick wanted to take me to eat. I said no. I wanted to go home. Then he got a wild idea to go to a disco. I didn't think we should. We went to the disco. I tried to talk Rick into bringing me home, but ten dollars stood in the way. Thank heaven the place closed, but it didn't help much. I had to have a hamburger. Am I ever glad to be here."

"Quite an evening." She nodded her head in understanding.

"What did I do wrong? Why wouldn't he bring me home?"

"He felt excited to be out with you, Linn. But, you're in control."

"How?" Had I had the power to be in my bed at midnight, nothing could have stopped me.

"It's very simple. You say one word—*no*. That's all it takes."

"Takes more than that," I protested.

"You have to mean it."

"Mom, how could I be so dense?"

"You worry too much about Rick's feelings. If you'd called him and canceled the date, you wouldn't be so tired. After having no sleep for two nights, do you really think a date is wise?"

"No."

"Exactly, but your mom is soft, too. She let you go, and she should have said no."

"But then I'd be mad at you."

"And you'd be sleeping soundly right now."

"If I get mad, that's my tough luck. You know what's best."

"If Rick gets mad, is that his tough luck?" Mom questioned.

"It sure is."

"I think we both learned something tonight. Linn, don't worry me anymore. It's not fun." I kissed Mom on the cheek. The first time.

"I'll do my best. That means you don't have to worry—ever."

"Thank you, Linn." Mom put her arm around me, and we both walked to my room. I said good night, and she made a face at me and went to her room. Gosh, I guessed I had a better mom than most of my friends. She cared.

I wanted to sleep forever, but I rolled out of bed close to noon. Mom finished Saturday chores, and she asked Joel to dinner. I had never met him.

"You worried he won't like me?"

"No. The other way around," Mom admitted.

"What do you care if I like him or not? I'm only a kid."

"Linn, be patient with me. I'm learning how to be a mother. It's easier than I imagined, but it takes time to work out the kinks." Things *were* getting better.

After lunch we watched TV for almost two hours. Saturday matinee. The first time—we'd had a lot of firsts lately. It was a romance. We both got all wrapped up in this girl whose face was smashed, and she had it reconstructed and was more beautiful than ever, except she didn't look like herself. I was going in to change out of my pajamas when the phone rang. I went on into the bedroom and pulled off my pajamas and put on my jeans and T-shirt.

"Linn," Mom called, "it's for you."

I took the receiver from Mom. I hadn't bothered to put on my shoes, and my bare feet were cold on the kitchen linoleum.

"Hi," I said, and then I nearly dropped over.

"Hello, Linn." The voice was so familiar. I'd heard it every day for fifteen years.

"Grandma," I shouted. "Grandma!"

"How are you getting along, dear?"

"Oh, my grades have gone down some, but I have a neat art class that I already told you about, and I went to a dance. Last night I even went out on a date with one of the boys from my art class."

"Sounds like you're having a good time," Grandma said.

"You bet. How's Grandpa?"

There was a little pause before she answered. "He's getting better. His arthritis is acting up a bit since we've had some rainy weather the last week, but he manages to get the chores done."

"It sounded in your letter like Twilight is growing. I can't wait to see her."

"That's what I'm calling about, Linn."

"Well, Grandma, we might not make it down for Christmas vacation. You see, Mom has this friend, Joel, and he's pretty lonely without her. Mom needs to see him, too."

"Linn, I thought if you'd like—and your letters sounded as if you wanted it—we thought you could come home. We miss you dear, and, well, we want you back."

Imagine. After two months she did call to tell me to come back, after all the nights I cried and felt bad and dreamed about brushing Starlight and romping with Twilight. And Grandpa—he hadn't written. I missed him most of all. Now I could go back to Pepper Hill.

"Grandma, could I talk to Grandpa for just a minute?"

"Surely, dear." I heard some murmurings of voices in the background, and then Grandpa came on the line.

"Hi, tadpole." The voice was deep and gruff like I remembered.

"Grandpa." I couldn't help the tears. My feet were so cold I sat on the kitchen table and put my feet on a chair. "Grandpa, I miss you something awful."

"I miss you, too. You behaving yourself?"

170

"Pretty much. You'll have to ask Mom about that."

"Her letters say you're minding."

"I try, but I get in trouble anyway," I confided.

"You coming home, partner?"

"That's what I wanted to talk about. Grandpa, I lived with you for fifteen years and loved every minute of it."

"Think you better stay with your mom, youngster?" Like I said, my grandpa was pretty smart. He knew how things were.

"She needs me, Grandpa. If she'll have me, I want to stay. You see, we're just starting to get acquainted. That might sound strange, but it takes time."

"Sounds like you're growing up, Linn."

"Don't call me that."

"Can't call you tadpole when you're a lady."

"I don't mind."

"All right. I'll keep your ponies fed until you get down here."

"I'll try to make it in the summer. Maybe I can get a job to pay the bus fare."

"I'll be looking for you. See you, tadpole."

"Bye, Grandpa. Can I talk to Grandma?" After a little space Grandma came back on the line.

"Hello, Linn. I heard your decision. You're going to stay."

"If Mom will have me. She can teach me a lot, and she cares about me. And I kind of like her, too." I looked at Mom, who was sitting on a chair in the kitchen. We smiled at each other.

"Linn, I'm sorry I ever suggested you leave

Pepper Hill. Please forgive me. I made a terrible mistake. I'm an old fussbudget, and I don't know how I ever thought you'd be a problem."

"No, Grandma, you did the right thing. I needed to learn to take responsibility better, but most important, I needed my mother."

"Are you sure, dear?"

"We'll argue sometimes, and we'll get mad, but we belong together."

"Linn, you're a lucky girl. So many people love you."

"Thanks, Grandma, I love you, too. Do you want to talk to Mom?"

"Please, dear."

"Okay. I'll see you." I handed the phone to Mom. I couldn't believe myself. Everything I'd wanted, and I turned it down. Mom didn't talk very long, but she said several times not to worry, that we'd be down whenever we got the chance. I guess Mom had changed, too.

When Mom hung up, I got worried. What if she didn't want me? "Is it okay? For me to stay, I mean."

Mom's face crumpled, and she started to cry. She folded her arms on the table, laid her head on her arms and cried more. I patted her shoulder, but didn't know what to say. She lifted her head and sniffed. When she looked at me, tears were all over her face. She grinned and held out her arms. I threw my arms around her, and we hugged each other. I started to cry, too. Mom didn't ever say I could stay, but I understood.

12

What a good day: test week over and no school-work on my mind. Mom and I felt more relaxed with each other, and I had made the decision to stay. A coming-of-age celebration, marking my letting go of the past and looking to the future, would be neat. Shakes at Arctic Circle! Could you believe I really want to see the place again after last night?

I hurried into the kitchen and picked up the phone to dial Patty. Mrs. Varow answered.

"Hello."

"Hi, Mrs. Varow, this is Linn. Is Patty around?"

"No, she isn't, Linn. She went roller skating."

"Oh, who with?" I felt dejected to think she left me out.

"A boy named Rick. Isn't he a friend of yours?"

"Yes, Rick Adams." I couldn't believe what I heard.

"He said something about your not having staying power and wanted Patty to take the second shift."

I couldn't help laughing. "Mrs. Varow, I got home this morning at three. I'm half dead. I hope Patty does better than I did."

"My goodness, that's a little late."

"I know. Mom and I went over that. I slept most of the morning. I didn't think Rick would get out of bed for a week. Roller skating. Why, he can't walk straight, let alone roller-skate."

"Apparently, he plans to try. He said he'd found this new burst of self-confidence. Really a charming boy."

"Yes, if you've had a good night's rest before trying to keep up with him. Would you tell Patty I called?"

"I will. They said six, but from what you're saying, I better leave her dinner in the oven."

"Thanks."

"Good-bye, Linn."

Patty was gone. Mom wouldn't want to go over there; it was too fattening. Wouldn't hurt to ask, though.

"Mom. Mom?"

"In the bedroom."

"Do you want to go over to Arctic Circle for shakes?"

"Linn, Joel's coming to dinner."

"All right."

"I've got to run down and do some shopping. Would you clean up the kitchen while I'm gone? Maybe you better run the vacuum again."

"Mom, you did it this morning."

"I know, but I want things nice."

I grinned at her. "You're acting like a lovesick kid," I said teasingly.

"Just clean the kitchen and keep your observations to yourself, Miss!" my mother said smartly, but I could see that she was restraining a smile as she turned to reach for her purse.

The house was pretty quiet after she left. I got through the kitchen work in no time. I even whipped up a cake from a ready mix before throwing myself into cleaning the living room. An imaginary picture of Joel drifted in and out of my mind as I worked. When I had finished, I wound up the cord and rolled the vaccum into the closet. The couch looked so shabby I decided to spread the afghan from Mom's bed over the worst holes. I was just surveying my work when I heard a bump at the door. It was Mom, loaded down with two heaping bags of groceries. I grabbed one.

"I thought I'd never make it." She sighed as we set them on the table.

"This ought to be some dinner. What time's he coming?"

"About eight."

"We'll starve by then," I protested.

"He has to work late and then go home and change. It takes time," she said, and started putting the groceries away in the refrigerator and cupboard. "Kitchen looks nice," she added on one trip.

I resigned myself to the long delay. I hoped he would appreciate the sacrifice. My curiosity to see him made the wait more frustrating.

Mom and I worked side by side for the better part of an hour getting everything set, even though dinner was hours away. Finally Mom said she was going to lie down for a nap. She wanted to be at her best. So there I was again, alone. I went to Mom's bedroom.

"Mom?"

"Yes, dear?" I think she was half asleep already.

"I'm going to take Dougie over to the Arctic Circle, to hold me over until dinner."

"Be back by seven."

"I will." It seemed as though Dougie and I had a lot more in common than I thought. We both had a hard time finding playmates. I really wasn't lonely for any friend. I needed to keep busy so I wouldn't think about Steve. Seeing him in class would be hard; worse, though, not to see him at all.

My cake frosting had turned out perfect, and I cut the layers in half so it would be a four-layer cake. I put the cake in the saver and washed up. Dougie would be surprised when I came over. I knew he would dance around for joy, and he didn't disappoint me.

"I want a brown topper," he sang as we walked along.

"Dougie, they're always such a mess. Why don't

you have a shake?" Might as well talk to a wall. He didn't care how much ice cream was in a shake compared to a topper.

"I want a brown topper," he insisted.

"Have one, but take napkins to wipe up all the drips." Last time, chocolate had smeared his mouth and had dripped down his shirt and his arms to his elbows.

We were almost to Ninth when a black car slid to the curb beside us.

"Steve!" Dougie screamed as if he hadn't seen him in a year, much less a week. Dougie ran to the car door, and Steve leaned over and opened it. I felt like rushing over, too, but I waited back on the sidewalk, wondering what to do.

"Where you going?" I heard the question from my position at the edge of the grass.

"Over to Arctic Circle. Want to come?" Little Dougie could never imagine that I would hate to have his favorite cousin along.

"You bet. Hop in."

"Hurry, Linn," Dougie called. "Steve's taking us." I stood, not knowing what to answer. I rubbed my hands up and down my jeans as I searched for something to say. "You coming?" Dougie waved impatiently. My feet didn't move, and I stared dumbly.

One minute I stood gaping; the next, Steve jumped out of the car and had his arm around my waist. "The car's over here," he explained. He pushed me along, and I eased inside, sharing the bucket seat with Dougie. Steve closed the door behind me and went around to the other side. As soon as he sat at the wheel, Dougie started in again.

"Steve, can I have a brown topper?"

"Whatever it takes."

"Oh, boy."

"What are you having, Linn?" Steve glanced over at me, and my voice died. I shrugged.

"I'll have a brown topper, too," Steve mulled. "I was at Karlene's, and she said the two of you headed this way. I thought I'd come along. You don't mind?"

"Heck no," Dougie piped up. "We love it. Don't we, Linn?" I couldn't help smiling then. Steve smiled, too.

"Linn probably got too many bruises the last time we played football."

"Don't worry, Steve. She's tough. Smashed a mouse with a broom handle."

"Dougie," I moaned.

"Such feats of bravery need to be rewarded. Linn can have double whatever she wants."

"That happened months ago, and you're not to mention it, Dougie. Especially when we're going to eat." Steve started to laugh. "And what's so funny?" I demanded as I swiveled to face him.

"That would make a good subject for a sketch— fierce determination, a beady eye taking aim . . ."

"The two of you are awful," I said. By this time Steve parked, and Dougie danced up and down as we walked inside.

"What'll it be, Linn?" Steve waited expectantly.

"Vanilla shake," I said as I fished in my jeans for my money.

"No, this one's on me—for our brave heroine." My eyes rolled toward the ceiling as I pulled Dougie toward a booth, and we sat down.

"Steve's swell," Dougie boasted.

"Yeah, a regular superhero all right," I said as Steve came and sat opposite.

"What made the two of you decide to come over here on a cold November day?" Steve asked as he switched caps on the salt and pepper shakers. Dougie immediately removed the caps and put them back to their original positions.

"Linn asked me," Dougie said absently. He couldn't get one of the caps to screw down. Steve took it off and motioned for him to have another go at it.

"So how come?" Steve turned melting eyes in my direction.

I hesitated to share my inner glow. "A welcoming party for me."

"To what?" Steve asked, now gazing at me intently.

"Salt Lake, my permanent home," I said with satisfaction.

"You're going to stay." His voice was quiet.

"Uh huh."

"Of course she's staying. She's my friend. Lives next door to me. Where else would she go?"

"Nowhere, sweetheart," I said, giving him a little squeeze.

"Don't do that. Girls get too mushy."

179

"I hadn't noticed," Steve said as his flashing eyes wandered back toward me. Luckily, the girl came with our order because I didn't know what to say, as usual.

When she set the ice cream down, I began to laugh. Two brown toppers and two vanilla shakes. I could barely eat one. The toppers had melted a bit already, but Dougie didn't seem to mind as he bit off the top and began to suck the ice cream. Steve managed his in three bites, adroitly holding it between two fingers and tipping his head back to pop the last of it in his mouth.

I turned my head away because Dougie already had a ring of chocolate around his mouth. Steve made no move toward the shake, so I pushed it to him.

"Better eat this, too, or it'll go to waste." He shook his head negatively. "I command you to eat," I said with a flourish of my hand.

"In that case." He took a spoon and began to eat. He had the nicest hands. They were tan, with little black hairs on the backs of his fingers—I stared down at the table for fear he would catch me staring at him. Out of the corner of my eye I saw Dougie wading into his ice cream.

"Dougie," I wailed. I grabbed three napkins out of the holder and began scrubbing the ice cream from his face and shirt.

"Give the poor man a chance," Steve protested.

"Yeah," Dougie echoed. "Give the man a chance."

"I'm giving you a chance to finish that cone right

now and be quick before you're covered," I said sternly. Dougie went back to slurping on his cone, and I shuddered.

"Say, how would you two like to come to my place and play some video games?" Steve asked.

"Can we?" Dougie asked eagerly.

"I have to be home by seven."

"We'll make that easy," Steve assured me.

"I'm going to play Radar and Rockets," Dougie announced.

"I've never played before," I admitted.

"That's all right," Dougie said. "I'll teach you."

"Gee, thanks."

"Better watch him, Linn. He'll beat the socks off you. He does it to me every time we play."

"You beat me lots," Dougie denied as he stuffed the last of his cone in his mouth. I could see why Dougie loved Steve. Even losers felt good around him.

We finished up and put our cups and napkins on the tray. Steve emptied them in the trash on our way out.

We stopped at Steve's house, an older, two-story red brick. The carefully pruned shrubs and newly painted trim on the eaves and around the windows showed somebody cared. Stepping stones lined the pathway to the door.

As we stepped inside, I glanced curiously around. I discovered a formal dining room off the hallway, opposite the living room. Steve led the way straight to the back of the house to the family room. He drew the drapes closed against the chill of the evening. Dougie ran to set things up. Steve turned to me.

"You look tired, Linn. Why don't you go upstairs and rest while Dougie and I play the first game."

"I'm fine," I said.

"Come here." He took my arm and led me back to the entry where steps went to the second story. "My room is the one on the left. Lie down for a few minutes."

"No." My chance to use Mom's advice. "I prefer to watch you two. I'll catch on quicker."

"No arguments," Steve commanded, and he pushed me up the first step.

"I said, no." Our eyes were on a level, mine stubborn and his compelling.

"Come on, Steve," Dougie yelled.

"In a minute," Steve called back, but his eyes never left mine. "Hey, this once do as I ask," he whispered.

"No."

"Please." I wasn't giving in to such a crazy request. "If that's how you want it," he said with resignation as he bent and put his shoulder to my waist. I didn't realize what he had in mind until he grasped my legs and lifted me off my feet.

"Put me down," I said angrily. I didn't want Dougie to run out and find us.

"Always the hard way, Linn," he said as he trudged up the stairs. He climbed without effort. I didn't kick for fear we'd both tumble down the steep steps. He pushed open a door and flicked on the light. Next I fell into a soft mound of velvet. He left before I lifted my head. The slow undulations of his water bed went totally unappreciated as I pushed up on my elbows.

My own face, gazing back at me from the wall from a saucy figure decked out in a blazer and faded jeans, cut short my sigh of exasperation. A brown cap replaced the baseball hat, and my long braid hung over my shoulder. The impish grin pleased me. Even more, the texturing with pastels blending blue, red and brown on the jacket gave an illusion of roughness. The creases in the jeans caused by my broad stance appeared real. I stared and stared. Me on Steve's wall!

I lowered myself flat on the bed and continued to stare through squinted eyelids. The waterbed lulled me. Something on the ceiling caught my attention, and I glanced up to check. My eyes nearly burst from their sockets.

On the ceiling. I couldn't believe it—on the ceiling . . . I didn't think I should ever recover . . . on the ceiling was an oil painting. Yes, of me, in a black negligée, lying on a grand piano. My hair shone as it spilled down over my shoulders and made two pools on the black surface. I couldn't believe it. He had painted my face with makeup. The eyes drooped; the mouth pouted.

I giggled out loud. How silly of him to put the thing on the ceiling! My gosh, the last thing he saw at night and the first thing he saw in the morning was me. Chari would kill him—or me—or both of us.

183

I couldn't help lingering on the velvet cover and taking in every detail. Line, perspective, balance, harmony, tension—everything was perfect. A warm feeling for Steve crept over me. Together we had accomplished a work of art.

I must have been in his room a long time because I heard footsteps on the stairs. I jumped off the bed and started out of the room, flicking the light switch as I went. We met as I started down the stairs. Steve stopped me. I grasped the carved wooden railing, but he removed my hand and lifted both my hands to his shoulders.

"See anything you like?" he murmured as his own hands rested just below my waist, on my hips.

"How can I tell you? Both are perfect in every detail. I can't decide which I like better. They're completely different."

"I enjoyed doing both of them."

"Even the piano one? How come you did that?"

"Don't you know? You were sensational." My mouth dropped. "Ever hear of jealousy? I didn't want anyone else to see you that way."

"I don't know about your father, but I bet your mother would have spanked you for putting it on the ceiling," I said severely.

"No, she wouldn't. She'd have laughed."

"I couldn't help laughing, myself," I said with a grin, even though it made me nervous to stand so close to Steve and feel the warmth of his skin through his shirt. After a long time he spoke.

"Linn, I care about you," he whispered. My ears couldn't believe what they heard. "I've cared a long time. Forever."

"But you can't." My heart pounded so loud I was afraid he could hear it.

"I do."

"I already told you how crazy I am about you," I said, dropping my eyes in embarrassment.

"Hey, I'm up here," he said, and his hand released me to move up to my chin. My lips trembled as he tilted my head back so I would have to meet his gaze. Gently, he brushed my lips with his. He drew me to his chest. "Steve, we can't do this. What will Chari say?" I protested.

"I dropped her before the Girls' Dance. That same night she got the chicken pox. That's why she told her friends I could go to the dance without her."

"Poor Chari," I said without remorse as my arms tightened about his neck.

"She has several guys lined up already," he murmured as his lips grazed my cheek. He pulled away, and we smiled at each other. Then he kissed me again. Just like my dream!

He hugged me, and we walked down the stairs with arms linked. Dougie waited at the bottom of the steps.

"You take too long."

"Sorry, old pal. Time to get in the rocket. Did you turn the set off?"

"Linn hasn't played yet," he objected.

"She has to get home," Steve explained as we reached the bottom step.

"She's just a girl, anyway." Dougie sighed.

"That's what I've been finding out."

"You aren't getting mushy?"

"Course not. Get in there and turn off the set."

"Right, captain." Dougie saluted and ran into the family room.

"I don't suppose you'd like to come to dinner?" I asked Steve. "I've made velvet cake and heavenly frosting—"

Steve grinned. "I'd love to. Dad's out of town for the weekend." He opened the front door. "Come on, Dougie, we're going to heaven," he called.

Not exactly heaven, I thought, but better than I had ever imagined. Much better.

First Love from Silhouette

THERE'S NOTHING QUITE AS SPECIAL AS A FIRST LOVE.

$1.95

First Love from Silhouette

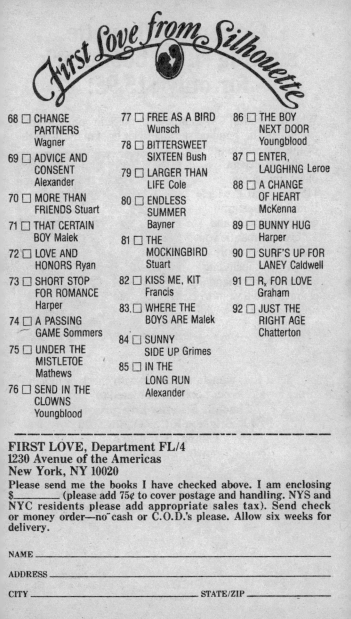

68 ☐ CHANGE PARTNERS Wagner

69 ☐ ADVICE AND CONSENT Alexander

70 ☐ MORE THAN FRIENDS Stuart

71 ☐ THAT CERTAIN BOY Malek

72 ☐ LOVE AND HONORS Ryan

73 ☐ SHORT STOP FOR ROMANCE Harper

74 ☐ A PASSING GAME Sommers

75 ☐ UNDER THE MISTLETOE Mathews

76 ☐ SEND IN THE CLOWNS Youngblood

77 ☐ FREE AS A BIRD Wunsch

78 ☐ BITTERSWEET SIXTEEN Bush

79 ☐ LARGER THAN LIFE Cole

80 ☐ ENDLESS SUMMER Bayner

81 ☐ THE MOCKINGBIRD Stuart

82 ☐ KISS ME, KIT Francis

83 ☐ WHERE THE BOYS ARE Malek

84 ☐ SUNNY SIDE UP Grimes

85 ☐ IN THE LONG RUN Alexander

86 ☐ THE BOY NEXT DOOR Youngblood

87 ☐ ENTER, LAUGHING Leroe

88 ☐ A CHANGE OF HEART McKenna

89 ☐ BUNNY HUG Harper

90 ☐ SURF'S UP FOR LANEY Caldwell

91 ☐ R$_x$ FOR LOVE Graham

92 ☐ JUST THE RIGHT AGE Chatterton

FIRST LOVE, Department FL/4
1230 Avenue of the Americas
New York, NY 10020

Please send me the books I have checked above. I am enclosing $_____ (please add 75¢ to cover postage and handling. NYS and NYC residents please add appropriate sales tax). Send check or money order—no cash or C.O.D.'s please. Allow six weeks for delivery.

NAME _____

ADDRESS _____

CITY _____ STATE/ZIP _____

Genuine Silhouette sterling silver bookmark for only $15.95!

What a beautiful way to hold your place in your current romance! This genuine sterling silver bookmark, with the distinctive Silhouette symbol in elegant black, measures 1½" long and 1" wide. It makes a beautiful gift for yourself, and for every romantic you know! And, at only $15.95 each, including all postage and handling charges, you'll want to order several now, while supplies last.

Send your name and address with check or money order for $15.95 per bookmark ordered to
Simon & Schuster Enterprises
120 Brighton Rd., P.O. Box 5020
Clifton, N.J. 07012
Attn: Bookmark

Bookmarks can be ordered pre-paid only. No charges will be accepted. Please allow 4-6 weeks for delivery.

N.Y. State Residents
Please Add Sales Tax

First Love from Silhouette

Coming Next Month

Heavens To Bitsy by Janice Harrell

Stu Shearin was definitely not Bitsy's type. He was too macho; he was always making inappropriate jokes; he drove too fast. He had at least twelve major faults and quite a few minor ones. Why then, couldn't she forget him once and for all?

Research For Romance by Erin Phillips

Becky loved working in the library. The only problem was that so far the only males who had ventured through the doors were either over sixty or under ten. Until one Saturday afternoon . . .

Lead On Love by Nicole Hart

When Anne went to Virginia to stay with her mother and new stepfather, she found out that all that everyone ever talked about was horses. Horses! Why should she care about *them*, even though the most attractive boy she had ever met just happened to be a star rider . . .

South Of The Border by Dawn Kingsbury

Artis was always telling everybody how madly in love she was with her Mexican pen pal, Manuel. Now she was going to meet him in person! The suspense was almost more than she could bear!